of slaves now sheltered by the islanders, who paints pictures and builds elaborate sand castles. Ezekiel's current picture, a terrifying vision of apocalypse, and a shipwreck during the storm lead grief-stricken Peter to make a terrible demand of God.

This novel is rooted in a unique, real landscape and based on a clear understanding of the accommodations that men living close to nature must make. The characters, though bearing surnames familiar in the area, are the author's creation. James R. Nichols, first a visitor to the islands, returned and returned, drawn by the folklore and character of the Outer Banks.

Nichols, a native of Troy, N.Y., graduated from Union College and spent four years in the Marine Corps as an intelligence officer. He earned his advanced degrees at the University of North Carolina and is now a member of the faculty of Muskingum College in New Concord, Ohio.

# Children
of the Sea

# Children of the Sea

by JAMES R. NICHOLS

JOHN F. BLAIR, Publisher
Winston-Salem, North Carolina

813.54
N619c
c.2

Copyright © 1977 by JOHN F. BLAIR, Publisher
Library of Congress Catalog Card Number: 77-20046
ISBN 0-89587-001-0
Printed in the United States of America
by Heritage Printers, Inc.
Charlotte, North Carolina
All rights reserved

Library of Congress Cataloging in Publication Data

Nichols, James R  1938–
  Children of the sea.
  1. Outer Banks, N.C.—History—Fiction.  I. Title.
PZ4.N6186Ch    [PS3564.I264]      813'.5'4      77-20046
ISBN 0-89587-001-0

*to*

"a"

# *Foreword*

ON OCRACOKE ISLAND, in the Wahab-Howard family cemetery, there are six stone monuments in a row. They memorialize a man, his wife, and their four children, all of whom died before their parents. Other than that and a great deal of restructured natural and social history, all the persons and events herein are fictitious.

There was a Job and there was a Pharaoh, both on the Outer Banks and in the Bible. There were Wahabs, Howards, and Farrows on the Banks. There were Arabs and pharaohs and kings in Egypt and the Near East. But there was never a King Job Pharaoh Wahab. He never lived.

This entire story developed out of a first glimpse upon that row of sand-hewn, moss-covered graves, the writing on which I could initially only guess. I have since then visited the Outer Banks many times. Most of the stories and folktales herein are still actually told, although I have taken the liberty to change centuries and names, to exaggerate, combine, and restructure actions as fictionally necessary. I have also added stories and tried to develop in Peter's character and personal revelations a mixture of both Old and New Testament traditions. The quotations and paraphrases of the Old and New Testaments, the Psalter, the Talmud, and the hymns are not necessarily intended to be exact but indicative of the perceptions of the individual characters and of the moral and intellectual lives that they led.

The Outer Banks, off the North Carolina coast, are among the most severely beautiful places on earth. They admit to no compromise and, I suspect, will eventually defeat and send in confusion all the shabby, neon, summer glitter with which present-day admen are burdening them. As it is, there are still some islands without bridges and roads. They are part of the

National Seashore, and thus the salesmen cannot yet reach them.

All the persons and central events herein are fictitious or legendary, but once upon a time, there were men and women who lived alone on these islands, and their children and their children's children unto countless generations.

# I

# PROLOGUE

OFF THE EAST COAST of the United States lie a group of islands, sandbars, and banks that stretch their tenuous and strangely dismembered fingers along the North American shore from the southern tip of Virginia, past North and South Carolina, until they end abruptly and arbitrarily long before what, if extended outward into the sea, would be the Georgia state line. Thus, Georgia cannot claim the chain to be her own, but if you visit the islands alongside any of the other three states, they will variously be described as part of the Virginia Tidewater, the North Carolina Outer Banks, or a northward extension of the South Carolina vacation coast, although none of the islands proper are within that state. In truth, the islands belong to no one. Lonely and isolated, they have passively ignored the more aggressive insularity of their stepmother states and learned instead to abide the woman whose children they most truly are—the sea.

To the north, the islands begin to thread themselves southward and eastward from the Virginia Banks at the southern end of Chesapeake Bay. They are the seaward wall of once rich alluvial lowlands whose faded red sands and clay stand raw and barren for thirty miles between the Great Dismal Swamp and Virginia Beach. The swamp itself circumscribes an oblong reach of land some twenty miles across and fifty miles long, obscurely resembling a hand pressed flat against the soft, moist earth with its huge, ungainly fingers intruding into the northeastern tip of North Carolina along either side of the Pasquotank River, through Camden and the Currituck, past Elizabeth City, and westward into the Chowan, until it, too, dark and viscous like some deeply sad, regrettable bruise upon the land, is covered by the more profoundly soft waters of Albemarle Sound. The swamp sprawls perversely southward for nearly three hundred miles but is constantly broken by the innumerable rivers and sounds that form the inner coast of North Carolina. Progressively, the Great Swamp becomes the J. and M. Dismal Swamp, Lake Mattamuskeet, Pungo National Wildlife Refuge, Angola Swamp, Holly Shelter Swamp, and south of Wilmington and the Cape Fear River, Green Swamp.

To the east, the islands continue southward and help form

the wide, dangerously shallow sounds that divide them from the continent's mainland so irrevocably. Bodie Island is actually not an island at all but a long, incredibly thin neck of land which reaches down the coast from Virginia Beach for seventy miles. It succeeds in protecting Currituck Sound from the Atlantic Ocean only on the most benign and auspicious occasions. At other times, when hurricanes or nor'easters move up or down the coast, they gouge huge inlets across the shifting membranes of sand, and Bodie Island for months, sometimes years, is truly an island. The distinction, however, is largely academic, for many islands along the coast are technically not islands at all except for the rare occasions when they, too, change as the wind and the sea demand it of them. Such an island stands isolated by either sea or swamp, but whichever it endures, it is no less alone.

Towards the southern tip of Bodie are Kitty Hawk and Kill Devil Hills, where the Wright brothers made their first successful flight of an airplane in 1903. Then the island continues past Nags Head and Whalebone until Oregon Inlet separates it from the most famous of the Outer Banks' islands —Hatteras. Today this area and Virginia Beach are major vacation spots with smiling, white-toothed salesmen hawking ⅛-acre building lots from June through August every year. But at the turn of the nineteenth century, the sand and grass stretched, constricted and skeletal, past small towns like Chicamacomico, Waves, Salvo, Kinnakeet, Buxton, and Frisco, all precarious and unnoticed beside the sea. Even now, from late fall to early spring, the area ceases all activity, grimly shuts itself in, and conserves its remaining energy to endure the harrowing of winter.

Near the town of Hatteras, the southern United States seacoast reaches its easternmost point, almost touching the northward rush of the Gulf Stream, which, not thirty miles offshore, is arrested and rudely forced eastward by the angry, cold waters of the Labrador Current. Because of this, the town of Hatteras was at one time a great fishing and whaling village and, before the Civil War, pretended itself a great entry point for ocean ships sailing into Pamlico Sound and then to the inland Carolina ports of Elizabeth City, Washington, and New Bern. The Sound's shifting floor, however, has always proved too shallow and too undependable to suffer an ocean-going trade. As Newport News and Norfolk to the north and Wilmington to the south grew into great ports, Hatteras declined into a sleepy little vacation village with its famous lighthouse marking the Diamond Shoals, which jut eastward like a knife fifteen miles into the sea.

The area has always been a vast graveyard of ships and seamen. The sharklike teeth of the shoals have torn the bottoms from untold ships that sailed too near land and the lighthouse during a storm. With their ceaseless, spumy fury, the shoals are the most dreaded and vigorously feared region in the Atlantic.

But the ships were forced to come north. There was no avoiding it. They followed in the wake of the current and ran before the sweep of the wind. By 1879, there were built between Currituck Beach and Cape Fear over twenty lifesaving stations in a vain and heroic attempt to divest the sea of its plunder. The deceptive undertow and currents along the beaches are extremely dangerous, and only the most careful and hardy of seamen can brave a storm successfully.

Below Hatteras, the Banks jut sharply westward into a long southern arc formed by Ocracoke Island, Portsmouth Island, and the Core Banks. These are truly some of the most lonely and timeless places in the world. Presently, there is a free hourly ferry between Ocracoke and Hatteras, but not long ago Ocracoke could be reached only on a weekly run, and the vague, sandy path that stretched down the islands to Hatteras disappeared on Ocracoke.

Ocracoke village had at one time entertained dreams of becoming a great entry port, but after the Revolutionary War, Ocracoke Inlet proved hazardous and undependable. So the town became sleepier and lonelier, and people in 1940 still called a fine, robust young man "beautiful," in the manner of the Elizabethan settlers who had so tragically attempted to establish Raleigh's colony on Roanoke Island further north. Portsmouth, Ocracoke's sister village across the inlet and a thriving port in the 1700s, even now is visited only once a week by boat. It is an island full of ill-fed, tick-infested cattle, and it too has no road at all.

To the south, Cape Lookout is at the ominous and angry tip of the Core Banks, and from there the islands move once again sharply westward and southward in a long arc along Onslow Bay to Wilmington and Cape Fear. There, a third arc repeats the pattern past the northern edge of the South Carolina coast. These islands are as profoundly silent as their northern cousins, and at night the fitful lights of tiny fishing villages pierce the looming monotony of the coast almost in despair. Only around Wilmington and in South Carolina have the beaches begun to be thoroughly exploited as tourist attractions. Largely, the Outer Banks remain in brooding silence throughout most of the year, separated from the rest of their world by dark, impenetrable lowlands and swamps which are at places over a hundred miles wide. The shallow sounds that they form marry with the Atlantic to insure that isolation as if nature herself were jealously and inexplicably guarding these, her inhospitable citadels.

The geological explanation for the Banks is more fascinating than terrifying. The coastal rivers of Virginia and the Carolinas were once more energetic than they are now and in earlier millennia deposited most of the deep loam and clay mixture that is so characteristically the soil of that region. These rivers also dropped great quantities of material on the edge of the North American continental shelf. To the north, the last ice age came and left, and the ocean lowered and raised. Eventually, the southward and northward rush of the Labrador and Gulf currents deposited coarse sand with the sediment and rolled the reefs landward to form the Banks. Consequently, a long and wide group of sandbars and shallows developed along the coast without the security of bedrock. Wells can be dug almost anywhere, and fresh water will invariably appear less than twenty or thirty feet down. During the 1940s, an oil company, on an ill-conceived adventure, drilled ten thousand feet into the sands of Hatteras and still had not hit a hard rock base when the crew finally abandoned the project.

Thus, the islands are at the constant mercy of the winds and tides which formed them. No one knows when or where a new inlet will be torn open or how long it will take for an old and seemingly established channel to fill with sand and prove unusable. Only the most expert pilots can safely guide the few large ships that still pass through the inlets and then over the wide, still waters of the Bank Sounds. In the summer these waters prove an excellent place for shallow-draft pleasure boating, but in the winter they become cold and gray, visited only by migrating birds and the nor'easters, which blow from November till March. Mostly the waters remain calm and imperturbable, exposing at ebb tide wide wastes of muddy, reddish clay sands which lie between many of the islands and at times reach for miles into the Sounds. Old-timers at Ocracoke talk seriously about the amazing ebb tide of October, 1894, when during the height of a hurricane, before the eye passed over the island, it was possible to walk the fifteen-odd miles over the bottom of Pamlico Sound between Ocracoke and Bluff Point on the mainland. No one tried it, of course, during the middle of a hurricane, and there is no record testifying to the validity of such claims; but the old-timers swear to it and maintain a penurious hold upon the mythology of the islands, demanding large payments of time and credibility from all those who would learn of the Banks. Yet, like the moneylenders in the temple, they, too, must eventually be cast out in order to gain an intimacy and palpable feeling for these islands. Eventually one must live on the islands in order to understand the terrible purgation that takes place upon them—the fearful cleansing that leaves a man as lonely and as vulnerable as the islands themselves, defenseless before the vicious and certain primacy of his physical environment and clutching desperately to the fluid, shifting sands of his own soul.

It is possible at such times to touch elusive history itself, to walk at Ocracoke where Captain Teach, Blackbeard, once walked and feel the awesome heaviness of his presence. Because of the very dangers of their shifting, undependable sands, the Outer Banks were a favorite center for pirates during the seventeenth and eighteenth centuries. Teach actually became a respectable man on Ocracoke and at one time commanded the loyalty and devotion of its citizens much more than did the British. There is still a deep water channel on the Sound side of the island, known as "Teach's Hole," and vacationers are inevitably directed to it, although they can stand forever beside the myrtle and yaupon, staring only across level water. Bush and scrub have reclaimed the area, and it is largely indistinguishable from the common ground. Except that Blackbeard did once walk there. It is enough that in such a lonely and forsaken spot a man tormented and perhaps insane, driven to senseless rage by the very senselessness of his own condition, which was not condition at all but feeling and act, there decided to become God and took the inevitable step to which loneliness and torment led him. And there he failed, as men without mercy and bereft of grace must inevitably fail. For if the islands teach us anything, it is in their abject diffidence and impoverishment. Then they are most poignant, most profound. They suffer themselves to be used and expended as the sea and her minion powers determine it.

Living things exist here timorously and only through constant compromise. Once, before the English settlers destroyed them through two centuries of misuse, there were great oak and cedar forests which ran the length of the Outer Banks and firmly anchored much of the islands' sands beneath them. The Banks easily supported much more wildlife than they do now, and small bands of Indians ventured into the lowland areas and even to the islands. Now that is largely gone. It was largely gone before 1800. Now ragged, taut wire-and-stick fences attempt to hold the sand in place as the oaks once did. The great flocks nest further inland in Tyrrell and Dare counties, and Pamlico Sound echoes with the hollow cry of those few birds and many gulls which still frequent the area, a more truly wild place than it ever was before.

The Sound remains beautiful only in its impertinent chauvinism, its impractical desire to remain itself without man and in spite of man. It, with its mother the sea and its father the wind, suffers intruders upon its ancient drama only unwillingly. Across the often no more than two or three hundred fragile yards of sand and grasses that painfully separate the quiet Sound from the turbulent Atlantic, man is neither wanted nor needed. The ocean tirelessly rolls up onto the land in long, sweeping, frothy waves of green water. Here and there a palmetto tree awkwardly attempts to discover the perverse logic of its new and strange home, but inevitably these are a sad and deformed species on the Outer Banks. Man put them there, and the winters are too cold to allow them more than temporary residence. Thus, they too suffer and abide. The shoals far out to the east continue to take their toll of ships foolish enough to hug the shoreline too closely, the islands continue to stretch themselves along the coast for nearly three hundred miles, the Sound shifts and changes with each storm, the swamps remain mosquito-ridden and impenetrable, and man seems unneeded within the pain and beauty of this timeless cycle.

Only hurricanes truly interrupt the slow continuity of change within which the islands especially insulate themselves. The storms move up from the south after a languid gestation of weeks, sometimes months, in the warm, fetid waters of the Caribbean. Then, during September, October, and November, they direct their wayward path north along the Atlantic coast, usually touching land at Cape Lookout and proceeding northward with inexplicable and savage fury over Cape Hatteras and into the colder reaches of the Atlantic, where they sicken and die.

For days preceding a hurricane, the normally spright, gay sea builds into dark, heavy swells, which roll and slap monotonously ashore from the south. The wind increases and cleaves deep rifts across the sand and into the grass-laden dunes. Houses are shuttered and boats tied down. The horizons become intensely gray. Solitary sandpipers, now awkward and tiny before the immense disinterest of the storm, course fitfully along the beach. A few palmetto trees stand naked and awry. The clouds thicken in a cavernous sky and rush to harrow the very loneliness that they have fathered.

Nothing stands before the terrible reality of the storm. Beneath its awesome power, only humility and mortification prove acceptable. Lights flicker and go out. The sea breaks contemptuously over the beaches. The grasses are beaten flat against the dunes. The islands themselves writhe as the storm strips them and rushes northward. The Atlantic shores are inundated by the rising water, and often entire mountains of sand disappear. All that moves does so at the behest of the wind. Men remain taut, shut up against the storm, praying that they may yet endure one more time. Only the tombstones survive the storm with equanimity. Silent and persistent, the wind is muted and benign when opposed by their equal eternality.

Inland at Bath, a strange story has attached itself to a lonely stretch of road which runs deep into dark woods about a mile west of town. Old Abraham Midgett used to tell the story to his children, waving his large, rope-gnarled hands over their heads as they sat at his feet and admonishing them in a deep, caliginous voice to ever bend before the Lord and his wishes, to worship and obey a God whose commands were as indelibly written upon the shifting sands of the Banks as they had been upon the tablets of stone that Moses brought down with him from the sacred mountain.

Abraham had been one of the roisterers in the dank gloom of that woods one Sunday eve during the holidays. He had been visiting his uncle and was planning to return the next day to Hatteras for Christmas. At church, Jesse Elliot invited him to join a group of young men who raced their horses in the wood. Racing and gambling on Sunday was a profane act, Abraham knew, but he was young, the day clear and crisp with a hard, cold sunlight shimmering off the pines, so he decided to attend the afternoon revels in spite of his misgivings. What happened later Abraham never forgot. The youths raced all afternoon, betting on this horse, then that. At one time Abraham had lost two dollars, but by four o'clock he was fifty cents ahead. This was the exact cost of the brandy he had brought with him to mellow the afternoon, which was unexpectedly building toward an evening storm.

Then it was decided to have one last race between Abraham and Jesse Elliot. Neither man's horse had lost a race, and it was agreed that the winner of the contest would certainly be the owner of the finest mount in the district. Dave Burris, more than a little drunk, had snickered at that and agreed that a mount, if not ridden well, was hardly worth its cost. The race began, a mile, twice around the sandy road through the woods, finishing just beyond the pines in the dying sunlight of an open field. Both horses were tall and strong. Jesse's, however, was a slender bay mare whose spirit was unable to match the superior strength and power of Abraham's three-year-old gray stallion, which immediately took the lead and steadily widened it throughout the race.

Then, on the second time around the far turn, Abraham heard Jesse yell in frustration to his mount, "Damn me, take me in a winner or take me to hell!" Abraham looked back in time to see the mare plant its hooves into the sandy earth and hurl Jesse over its neck into a nearby tree.

The racing path was a narrow one, and Abraham could not easily rein in his horse. He made a circuit of the woods again, stopping momentarily to tell his friends at the woods' edge to go for a doctor because Jesse was hurt. It did no good. When the other roisterers arrived, they found Abraham kneeling beside Jesse Elliot, who was dead of a broken neck. The mare had disappeared and was never found.

In front of the tree were five shallow impressions, the mare's hoofprints. They remain there to this day. Nothing has effaced them for close to a hundred and eighty years. Nothing grows in the prints. During hard rains, the sandy road has washed out numerous times, but the impressions remain, immutable within the somber gloom of the woods.

Years later, Abraham took to saying that he'd seen a dazzling ray of fitful sunlight tear sharply through the pines at the last second and embrace, in some corrosive, actinic hold, both man and horse. That, he maintained, accounted for the Devil's Footprints, as they were called, and Mark Eden, who arrived at the spot minutes later, swore on his deathbed that he heard a cry of pain out of the pernicious sky and saw a fading penumbra of unholy light over both Jesse and Abraham. Two days later, after the storm had broken and passed out to sea, Abraham returned to the road on his way home. There in the still-wet sand were five perfect hoofprints, but now of a horse large beyond imagination. Abraham always contended that the cry (if there was one, for he never heard it) was Jesse's pain at parting, the cry of youth, which, had it the choice, would not die and leave the Banks.

In any case, for years afterwards, preachers warned their flocks of the terrible dangers of breaking the Sabbath and flouting God's will. Old Abraham was never known to touch another drop of liquor. In time, some said that the woods were haunted by the ghost of Blackbeard, who had lived in Bath for a short time. The hoofprints had to be those of his horse, they said, as he vainly searched for his lost treasure.

Thus, the stories are as the islands and swamps, inconstant and impertinent. The gray morning seas roll in out of the fog and fall abruptly on the hard sand. The gulls swing in wide, afternoon arcs toward the sun and search for carrion along the wide stretches of beach which string themselves southward along the coast. At night the men return from the sea, and the sea itself is once again alone in the approaching darkness. The graves remain unvisited, except rarely by strange and new generations, and the shores are unfrequented except by the waves and what the sea brings them.

# II

# CONFESSIONAL

EZEKIEL SHAMBLED northward up the coast. Old Ezekiel, the last Negro upon Ocracoke at the turn of the century, silly in the head, who had for so many years been boy to the Midgetts up in Hatteras and later worked for Job "Pharaoh" Wahab, now walked easily in the brilliance of morning sunshine. All his life (he knew) he'd been a seeker (yes, of dreadful knowledge). But now, aged and gray, he recounted the old stories to himself as he walked.

His mother (now dead, but Ezekiel knew) was the onlyborn child of the Seven Sisters, all daughters of an African king, who were sent into slavery through avarice and deceit and who, after making the Middle Passage, were sold in Charleston to the Nixon plantation up Perquimans County way. Years later, when the tuberculosis spread through the county, Mr. Nixon manumitted the sisters and the other sickly Negroes on his plantation and sent them to a spot encircled by seven hills above Nags Head (seven hills, and holy they were). There they had all got well, and Ezekiel's mother was born to Deborah, the most beautiful of the sisters, who still possessed the emerald ring she wore at court upon the Niger (this he had been told and told himself many times).

Later, when the Lord had worked a miracle cure, most of the blacks returned to Nixon's, but Deborah hauled off down the Banks to the Cape and (because Miz Mary was laid up) took to work for the Midgett family. Ezekiel's mother was a young girl by that time, and so she (and later Ezekiel himself) stayed on right naturally. The years of work for Pharaoh seemed only a short interruption, one in which he learned to read (Pharaoh taught him) and to stack and sort cargo in the Ocracoke warehouses.

Then the war came. It had brought great misery to the people, but to himself it had brought only strange freedom. Afterwards (in love, not might), he'd been Midgett's nigger again, and it was in those years he'd begun to paint. Miz Mary let him do it, taught him how. She'd always had him help her clean up after her own work, but after Gabriel's return from the war she'd had a talk with her son.

"Oh, for heaven's sake, Gabe, leave me be," she'd said. "He's gittin' a bit silly now and it don't hurt. He's good for little else, and he is our nigger. Besides, he knows his colors."

Ezekiel laughed at that and looked out to sea over the dunes. No doubt nobody could make sense of it, but it didn't matter. Old Miz Mary knew (and so did he) the softness of the paints, their strange viscosity as you put them on the board, the liquid motions your hands could make with the brushes, and the great castles and cities you could build and shape with color way out to the edges of the board. The supreme excitement of surfaces and textures Ezekiel knew (and as he got older and older he knew even more). Miz Mary died and left her paints to him. The townsfolk just laughed as he got more and more touched (but Ezekiel knew and knew and waited for the empire to come). He'd smiled, too, that day Miz Mary died. Then he'd fingered his Bible and looked far out to the east over a clear, bright sea and blue sky to the horizon.

Today was fine and clear with warm morning sunshine sharply outlining the shadows that the sandbanks cast across one another. The gulls were out in great multitudes, and their shrill cries echoed plaintively through the air. Only the strongly gusting wind, which sometimes whipped the sea oats to the ground, and the massive banks of clouds building far out to the northeast intruded upon the otherwise benign calm of the morning. Like most islanders, Ezekiel always looked toward the northeast during the winter months, and it was bandied about the town that when he had been young old Zeke could smell a storm. Even now there were few who knew all the signs the way old Ezekiel did. He was quick to feel a change in temperature and air pressure. He knew when the wind was too sharp and erratic. Every morning he watched the tides and the waste they washed shoreward to learn if the sea had changed color. Often the fish, too, would leave the Sound and go out to sea (Ezekiel knew). Today was such a day, and Ezekiel didn't like it.

He looked far up the beach and saw a moving, black dot against the skeleton of the old *Home* (and a great storm it was that sank her). As he drew closer, the dot wavered, grew larger, acquired arms and legs, and became the loosely jointed body of Peter Wahab.

Mr. Peter, of course, thought Ezekiel, his friend, for no one else would come out here on such a windy, cold day. January was a time of persecution for the islanders. Like the nor'easter forming out to sea even now, the month brought retribution, the certain knowledge of pain and beauty, indistinguishable and arbitrary.

Ezekiel had seen such mystery many times before. Once a sandpiper had been gathering carrion before the swift waves of a gathering storm. He had watched its swift motions as it darted in and out, always inches before the waves. Then, abruptly, the bird bent its neck over a stubborn piece of dead crab buried in the sand. It failed to look up and was caught unawares by a mountain of white foam. The sandpiper flipped backwards and to its left into the water and then just lay amid the foam. The wave quickly dissipated into the sand, and Ezekiel thought the bird would get up and continue down the beach; but inexplicably it just lay there while the next wave bubbled over it, lifted and floated it further in to shore. He went to the bird and fondled it, only to find that it was dead. Somehow the bird had broken its neck. It should not have been (he knew), but it was. How terrible, how terrible and awful in God's will death was.

By now Ezekiel could see Mr. Peter clearly. About three hundred feet south of and behind the white man, he stopped and squatted down on the beach, thereby paying deference not only to the other man's privacy but to his old friend's chastening as well, for Peter Wahab, the first and only born son of Hosea Wahab, Pharaoh's no-account brother (and the last and best hope of the family in those early years), had been sorely visited as of late and was about to lose his own, last son to Old Man Death. Ezekiel scratched his white beard and threw his baggage of cans, hooks and line, brushes and paints, a pair of torn gloves, and assorted odds and ends beside him on the hard, wet sand. He took a large clam shell from the pile and began digging in the sand. Ezekiel wanted to build a castle, and as the old Negro went about his work, he muttered over and over to the wind the strange history of the Wahabs.

Ezekiel had been told (and he always listened carefully) of how old Wahab, an Arabian sailor (Lebanese, Turk, or Egyptian; folks never knew for sure) was washed ashore during the storm of 1825. His ship had been returning from Antigua with molasses and rum bound for London when the Diamond Shoals had ripped its keel from end to end with only the spare, young Levantine saved from the jaws of an angry sea.

Ezekiel stopped and watched Peter Wahab twirl his fishing line over his head in an ever-increasing arc until finally the hooks and sinker on its end were flung high over the breaking waves and into the sea. Ezekiel shook his head and returned to his castle-building. Mr. Peter wasn't a very good surf fisherman. He couldn't swing his line fast enough over his head, and his tackle never got far enough out over the waves. It looked as though Mr. Peter hadn't caught a fish all morning.

Ezekiel chuckled as he dug with the clam shell and remembered how, when they were children, Pharaoh had often taken them both fishing in the Sound, comforting them when they became impatient through the long hours of waiting with stories of the family. He had told of how old Wahab had married and had three children—Job and Hosea and Cassandra—and then lost his wife in the unsuccessful bearing of a fourth; of how within a generation the Wahabs had become great traders and stockmen upon the Banks; and of how (Ezekiel knew) old Wahab had offered up his wife, whom he had so dearly and shortly loved, to the very God who so capriciously and incommodiously had refused his own bewildered soul. Afterward, old Wahab had hated his wife (unreasonably so) for making him love her and then leaving him so callously.

"Jus' like you, Mr. Peter." Ezekiel broke into a low, audible voice before the wind. "He jus' like you. Hate the very folk that love him so. Only he didn't know it neither."

Ezekiel stared up the beach at Peter Wahab. What a strange man, strange and harsh, Mr. Peter's grandfather, who set his own sternness and sense of justice against the mercy and grace of God's own son. Old Wahab had denied the sovereignty of the islands, of the several humiliations which he had suffered at their hands.

Oh, those Wahabs were strange folk, Ezekiel thought. They'd done well. Old Wahab had married Ruth Parker; his first son Job—Martha Jenkins; Job's brother Hosea—Jenny Meekins; and their sister Cassandra—a Howard.

*Take ye the sum of all the congregation
of the children of Israel, after their families,
by the house of their fathers, with the number
of their names, every male by their polls.*

Yes! Yes! Bankers all and a good lot. All worthy sons of Abraham. They'd bred into the land, prospered as traders in Ocracoke, Portsmouth across the inlet, and even up to Hatteras and beyond. Eventually, the family had warehouses and land as far north as Elizabeth City and as far south as Cape Lookout and Morehead. Job, "King Pharaoh" in later years, had mostly done it, acquired the land and directed the family in business long after old Wahab had lost energy. And Pharaoh had sired one daughter—Judith, the sprightly girl with a luxuriance of black hair which fell in tangles upon her strong, full shoulders. But Martha had born to Job Wahab a daughter who could not accept the rigid, lonely life of the islands. And Judith had left.

> *The days of my youth thou hast shortened,*
> *thou hast covered me with shame. How long*
> *wilt thou hide thyself, forever?*

Job had walked the long, wave-racked shores and listened for the voice he knew must come, but it had not.

> *I will say unto the Lord, He is my refuge*
> *and my fortress: my God; in Him will I trust.*

He'd murmured between tightly closed lips as the water washed over his boots and fled back into the sea. Job's face, once unnaturally soft and almost effeminately light of complexion, weathered. Vast sears crossed his now ash red forehead, and he had become grizzled and old.

Ezekiel rose and stretched himself. He was grizzled and old (he knew), like the gray timber over yonder, the one with the shark's head, open mouthed, protruding from a large, warped knot in its side.

"Get 'em," he yelled, "get 'em, old Racer. Chomp 'em good." He bent down, rested his hand on his knees, and chomped his jaws as though eating.

The timber was a spar from a ship which had broken up on the beach during Racer's Storm. It had remained half-buried in the sand ever since, the shark slowly becoming ever more distinct, ever more able to frighten the infrequent visitor to the Banks with his cavernous, but forever toothless, mouth. Now and then young men would bring their girls here in order to comfort them after they jumped (in mock surprise) away from the wooden effigy.

"A toothless old man, that's all you are," Ezekiel chided.

Toothless, like Mr. Peter's father, who had died at seventy-two of smallpox contracted from the infected seamen of a ship that had put into harbor for two days to water and resupply. Hosea had died terribly and in agony, his nostrils distended, his face black and pustulated, and his lips drawn back across his rotting mouth in what seemed a vicious sneer, outrage and disbelief written upon his countenance. Hosea Wahab went to his grave with the suppuration from his nose still moist as it dribbled over his lips and mixed with the sweat of his chin and neck.

At the end, Job had been unable to stay in the room. The putrescence of his own brother's body overcame him. He walked out of the sickroom, where Jenny remained, down to the kitchen of the cottage; and alone with Ezekiel and Peter (sired late in Hosea's forty-ninth year), Job Wahab cried, not out of fear but out of anger and frustration—as he imagined his brother died out of anger. He put his large, knotted fists to his eyes and cried.

*The Lord liveth and blessed be my rock;*
*and exalted be the God of the rock*
*of my salvation.*

It was the cry of Job's father, old Wahab, at his own death fifteen years before, when, stumbling out of bed in a fever, he had lurched toward the Bible upon his dresser, his eyes wide and intense upon its worn pages, and, unable to support himself any longer, had caught the dresser's edge, fallen heavily to his knees, and died.

It was a natural thing, Ezekiel thought, to die. It was! Even the snow geese which returned each winter from the north in long, slow, arcing flocks, even they died. He looked back toward the Sound for a long moment and then checked his castle walls.

Mr. Peter had wanted no more than this. The islands. His sons. His wife. The cottage of his father to which he had so belatedly (when his mother died) brought his wife Rachel Payne, he forty and she eighteen years his junior. This was all he wanted. If Job, and Hosea, and old Wahab had died in bitterness and vanity, he would not. He had sold the lands up north and sold the store at Kinnakeet to one of Sandra's boys. The warehouse and store at Hatteras were sold to old Bob Howard.

*Vanity. All is Vanity,*
*Vanity and vexation of spirit.*

He'd kept only his books—from Hampton-Sydney, where Job and his mother had sent him for three years (four, if only he had consented to stay)—and a small share in the Ocracoke store, now owned by Gabriel Midgett and largely tended by his wife while Gabriel ran the lifesaving station. Such was all that Mr. Peter had left unto himself.

Now, Mr. Peter tended stock, the small, sturdy ponies of the island; fished in the Sound; and cared for his family—Rachel and Isaac. Often these days he walked the shore and felt the wind, stinging and cold upon his face. Like Ezekiel, he saw the tall cedars and pines bend beneath the wind's dominion. He watched the sands change and shift as the ocean bid them, and he knew that this was his home. And like the lone palmetto tree that Job had brought to the Banks when almost a seedling to beautify his sister-in-law's home, Mr. Peter (Ezekiel knew) wished to bend with the wind—to endure. But like Jonah in the whale, like old Wahab and Job "King Pharaoh" too, both orphaned within a foreign land with the mark of Cain upon their souls, like them Peter Wahab (though he knew it not) also wished to justify his God before man.

Yes, Mr. Peter was sorely visited of late. Three of his four children had died, all in the past two months, two in the past fortnight, and only last week his remaining eldest son was taken sick as well. It had been a terrible winter for the islanders (Ezekiel knew that). A great plague had been visiting Ocracoke since October last. It had (Ezekiel knew) struck almost every house in Ocracoke village. Death was hardly new or unusual on the islands; fishermen and seamen lived with death upon the shoals. The Banks themselves, usually free of the malaria that scourged the settlements across the Sound, had been visited by a warm, fetid summer. Young Bob Howard lost his youngest daughter, and old Gabriel Midgett's niece died as well.

All over the Banks the disease was prevalent, and people boarded and screened themselves in at night, sweating through the long, torpid summer and the fall which followed it. Like the white plague, tuberculosis, which was prevalent inland, the disease took a terrible toll upon the unprepared islanders. Ezekiel felt that some great wrong had been done to bring such affliction upon Ocracoke. His people were not a sickly lot. Stories were told of the great healthful qualities of the Banks. Old Daniel Howard lived ninety-six years before resting in the Lord's bosom; he even fathered old Bob Howard at fifty-four, old Bob Howard, who at ninety-two himself was still active and vigorous. Mr. Peter's grandfather, the first Wahab, had not died till he was eighty-three, long, long after his wife had left him alone with three young'uns.

That was why Mr. Peter's burden was so great. All his family was dying and he would be left alone. Thomas had not even a headstone for his grave. He'd died six days ago, leaving his mother upon her knees weeping at his bedside. James, Matthew, and Thomas, all dead. Ezekiel looked up again and strained to touch the heart of Mr. Peter. Surely it was a great trouble (he knew), but God never visited his children beyond his own love. Surely there were some words for the white man whose last child now lay sick with fever.

> *I have heard of thee by the hearings*
> *of the ear, but now mine eye seeth thee.*

Just then Peter Wahab's body jerked forward. Off balance, Wahab stumbled a few steps and fell to his knees, sliding a short distance over the sand on his left hip. Finally, he braced his feet in front of him and stopped, attempting to right himself. Immediately Ezekiel began running toward Mr. Peter. He knew what had happened, and he silently resented the stiffness in his aged muscles which prevented him from reaching his friend sooner. Mr. Peter had a big one on his line, Ezekiel was sure of it. In Banker fashion, Mr. Peter had tied the line loosely about his waist once he'd gotten a tug on it. The second pull on the line, however, must have been unexpectedly strong, and now the fisherman was in danger of being soaked in the cold surf before his feet could find purchase to pull against the fish. By the time Ezekiel reached Peter Wahab, his friend had slipped once more in the wet, unsubstantial sand near the surf. He was ankle deep in water and leaning hard against the line.

"Looks like you could use some help, Mr. Peter," Ezekiel yelled over the roar of the waves.

He had grabbed hold of the line, which Wahab had begun to coil, when another unexpected run by the fish sent both men sprawling to their knees. The water in which Peter Wahab had been standing had run out to sea now and Ezekiel and Peter fell only on sand, but it was wet and cold, and Ezekiel tasted its salty putrescence.

"Seems I do, just a mite," the white man yelled, laughing, surprised by Ezekiel's appearance.

Mr. Peter had come there (Ezekiel knew) early in the morning and had failed to notice the old Negro walking up the beach. "That there mus' be a shark for sure, Mr. Peter," he said.

Ezekiel gasped for breath as the men picked themselves up and pulled against the line. He realized that he was too tired from his long run to help much, but he strained against the fish's strength anyway and, together with Wahab, stumbled back out of the wash of surf about their feet, giving line as they went.

Then, almost as suddenly as it began, the battle ended. The line went slack.

"Watch it!" Wahab yelled. "He's running in." But their frantic work failed to help. There was only slack, slack line and lost fish, and Peter Wahab and old Ezekiel sweating before a stiff northeastern breeze. The two men stood for a long minute looking out to sea.

"Ah," said Wahab finally, "shark or no, we didn't play him enough, Zekiel. We didn't play him enough."

"That ole shark, he play us, Mr. Peter," Ezekiel admonished. "He was a big'un. Seems like to me that ole shark lost us rather than t'other way 'round."

Peter laughed again. The old Negro was probably right. Shark or no, it had been a fair fight, no doubt of that. Well, at least it would make a good fish story for Rachel. He grinned wryly. Then Peter noticed that Ezekiel was shivering and that their clothes were wet.

"Come on, Zekiel," he said, coiling the line into his hand and walking up the beach toward his gear. "We'll build us a fire over near the dunes and have coffee while we dry off."

Wahab turned away, and for an instant sunlight sparkled over Ezekiel's face, blinding him as it lit the sand with strange, wet fire. Ezekiel looked and thought he saw Peter's dead Uncle Pharaoh again, walking away from him, his skin seared and leathern, carrying himself stiff and unforgiving as he had that day he turned from Judith, his only child (a lost child—Ezekiel knew), and lost her not from accident or death but from rebellion. And Judith, he thought as he gathered his belongings and searched for firewood along the beach, Judith left and made Pharaoh's life doubly lonely in bitterness and despair.

Then the vision passed, and Ezekiel found himself sitting before a fire in the lee of a sand dune, and Mr. Peter, white-knuckled, gripping a cup of coffee.

"Ah, Ezekiel," Mr. Peter was asking casually, "why? Why, Ezekiel, didn't we get that old fish?"

"He a tough one fer sure, Mr. Peter, no doubt," Ezekiel responded dutifully.

Peter Wahab's shoulders slumped. "It's been a tough year."

"Yes it has, Mr. Peter. It sure 'nough has."

And this time Ezekiel saw old Wahab, Mr. Peter's dead grandfather, asking the same question, "Why?" upon his knees, his head pressed into the pew in front of him. "Why?" Even the congregation would sit in awed and silent reverence and whisper "Why?" Every Sunday old Wahab went to church and asked, his knuckles whitening as he gripped the back of Jeremiah Meekins's pew. And Job and Cassandra and Hosea went too (and in later years, their families in turn), and they bent their knees and asked "Why?" not really knowing why but asking nonetheless. Pharaoh later said it was because the letter of the old law was strict and plain, but the new law different and slippery. Old Wahab had wanted to bring God to answer for his mercy and grace. "Why?"

"Why didn't I catch you, old fish?" Peter suddenly stood up and tried to skitter a shell toward the water, but it hit sand and stopped. "Why's Isaac so sick? Why'd Pharaoh lose his only child? Why'd we make so much money? Why—?" Peter stared out beyond the waves and saw a school of porpoise playing in the vagrant sunlight. "Why'd you spit out my line,

Old Sal?" he mocked at the sleek, black bodies, remembering the island legend of a porpoise-woman. He bent down and threw a broken scallop shell far into the waves. "Why'd you spit out my line?"

Peter stared into the fire a moment, then turned to the rough and decayed skeleton behind him. He and Ezekiel had been friends since as a youngster Ezekiel had worked for Job and later for Gabriel, Abraham Midgett's son, who some twenty-five years ago had moved down from Hatteras to take over the Howard store. They had fished together often these last years, and Ezekiel helped out regularly with the stock. All those years....

"You remember this wreck, Ezekiel?" he asked.

"Why, sure do." The Negro's face brightened. He blinked his eyes as if coming back from a dream. "That's what's left of the old *Home*, for sure. Mus' be sixty years since she went down below the Cape."

"Closer to seventy, I reckon," Peter said. "She was a great ship in her time. The sea took the Rev. and Mrs. Buckner that day along with their only young'un." Wahab, Ezekiel saw, was talking to himself, walking over to the wreck and gripping a decaying rib until his knuckles whitened. "Pharaoh used to tell me how the ship ran aground off the Diamonds with close to sixty people clinging to the fo'c'sle as it broke off and was driven ashore. Right out there." Peter pointed seaward. "Job said out there not two hundred yards offshore she stood, her riggin' down, and she stove in and died with the breakers thunderin' over her and the storm poundin' her to pieces. Rev. Buckner and his wife just kneeled there on the fo'c'sle as it broke up, praying to God for deliverance with their young'un held fast between 'em, until finally a huge wave broke over them and they were gone. Never found, either. Next day bodies were lined up all along the shore and others floatin' in every hour. One woman had been lashed to a settee, and she was washed up alive, Lord only knows how; but she didn't live out the day. It was a fearful storm, that'un. Lord knows it was."

Peter stopped and continued to look out to sea. He didn't really expect an answer from the old Negro (Ezekiel knew); his place was to listen, to provide company when it was needed. "But the Rev. Buckner had died along with his whole family, and was he ever once told why? Was all that prayin' out in a wild sea within sight of a shore they could not reach, was it ever answered?"

Ezekiel stirred restlessly. He knew what was happening and he didn't like it. People always questioning him about the Lord's will—and white folks, too, who should've known better, askin' why and expectin' him to know. He watched a gull run quickly under an oncoming wave and catch up a bit of carrion before the wave broke. Always questioning. Miz Mary, Pharaoh too, so many years ago when he'd kilt—that nigger.

He remembered Deborah in her silence, the taut, thin hands, the almost whiteness of her knuckles as she cried to be let die. "Let Him come unto me," she'd said. "Let my Lord come unto me." Then she'd died. Why? Lord only knew.

Ezekiel propped an old piece of wood on his knees and began fumbling in his bag for some paints. He especially wanted that half-used can of red paint Garbriel had given him two days ago after they'd finished fixin' up the stock room. He wanted to paint the whole board and feel its fine smoothness. A crab scuttled across the sand; a willet shrieked high overhead. Ezekiel began to paint. He knew of men's labors; he had known so many years ago when everyone thought he was goin' a bit touched.

"Lord's will," he crooned. "Lord's will, Mr. Peter, Lord's will it was. Lord's will."

And the Lord's will it had been, too, when Job "King Pharaoh" Wahab had beaten that nigger, one of his slaves, in what was accounted still an inexplicable fit of anger. Pharaoh had tied the slave, a great hulking Negro with deep, intense eyes, to the twisted, serrated trunk of a live oak tree in his front yard. He had then doubled a wide leather belt and begun hitting the slave with the loose and buckled ends. He struck the bound man again and again, all the while oblivious to the loose ends of the belt, which he could not control and which were making long, red welts upon his own upper arm.

The Negro, nameless to this day (Ezekiel knew), had never cried out. His thick, black lips winced with each blow, and a thin, red line of foam soon appeared from the corners of his mouth. King Pharaoh had continued to beat him upon his back, head, and arms until, covered with the blood of his own raw, open wounds as well as Wahab's, the Negro slumped to his knees, still staring incredulously at the convoluted, wind-torn trunk of the oak, and fell unconscious. He did not fall to the ground, for the leather thongs which held his hands in wide, involuntary supplication had been affixed too high; and thus the Negro's torso hung suspended, oblivious to Wahab's disjunctive chanting, which continued long after the sharp, arhythmic strokes of the belt to which it had begun, ceased. "Ye shall not. Ye shall not. Shall not in my house. Ye will not."

The Lord's will. It was that way with King Pharaoh. The Negro could have tried to run away, stolen from the Wahab warehouses, or even attempted to rape Pharaoh's rebellious daughter Judith. No one knew and everyone talked. It was that way. The Lord's will.

Peter Wahab turned abruptly. It was as if the Negro had slapped him, stinging upon the face. Had he ever suggested that it was not? Had he ever failed to accept the Lord? What on earth did the old man mean, and who was he to question him? Didn't he know what had happened only six days ago, that Thomas had died? And now Isaac, Isaac his firstborn, his eldest who at fourteen was just about to become a man, now he too was so desperately ill. "God's will!" What did Ezekiel know of God's will, of a merciful and just God, of Jesus raising Lazarus from the dead and curing the sick? What did he know?

*If it is done unto the least of these
my brethren, it is done unto me.*

A gust of wind blew sand in Peter's eyes and he turned his face. As he wiped his eye with his sleeve he said, "Yes, Ezekiel, the Lord's will we know." The grasses swayed upon the dunes. "But God loves us all, don't you worry none." He would not let go in front of this old Negro, his friend whom he had known for so long. He could not remember when he had not known Ezekiel.

Ezekiel continued to paint the board. He shifted his weight from one buttock to the other. "Yes, Mr. Peter, that's for sure. The Lord loves us—I know—loves us all, especially those in need and trouble. Especially, He loved those people on the *Home* and took them into his bosom that night. I know He did, I know. He loves us all."

Ezekiel was growing more upset. Course it was so. Pharaoh knew that. Deborah knew that. Abraham and Miz Mary, even Gabriel, and Judith gone these many years, they all knew. But the paint was now all on the board, and he was busy deciding what color next should go up in the left-hand corner. Yes, that was where he should start, up there in the corner with the curious nick in the wood.

"Why, Lord even loved old Quork, Mister Peter," he continued. "Old Quork who went out in that awful storm so many years back. Bared his teeth, he did, at God's world and went to tend his nets in the Sound, all the time shoutin' heathen oaths at the men who stayed on the beach and begged him not to go. Out he went and the Lord loved him even then. He went, though. Blessin' us out as he went, even standin' up in his boat and wavin' his big knotty fist at us. Lord even loved him, and if'n hell didn't get him that night, the Lord must've surely taken old Quawk to his bosom. Quork, Quawk, Quawk." Ezekiel played with the sound.

"Yes," he was speaking faster now. He had squeezed some orange oil onto the corner and was trying to fasten it to the board with his palette knife. It was just the right color. He felt that now, a touch of sun in the fire. "Yes, old Quork may be out there still. The Lord giveth and the Lord taketh away."

Peter wiped his face and lips as the Negro spoke. Ezekiel had no right to say these things. He looked up at the sun, shaded now behind a thin cloud. It was getting on towards noon. It had taken him over an hour to walk up here. No knowing how long he'd stayed before Ezekiel arrived. He'd best be getting back to Rachel. Breakfast would be late enough this morning, and he'd already caused his wife sore worry. She would be fretting over him before long. He turned and began to walk down the beach when the worn sole of his boot caught in the sand. He bent down and neatly folded back the offending front edge. After two or three twists, he carefully ripped away the worn piece of leather. He held it in his hand and looked at it, then upon impulse threw it toward the ocean. The wind caught it, however, and the leather described awkward and invisible circle patterns in the air before it hit the dunes.

"Yes," said Ezekiel working and chanting over the old board, now grown bright with greens and yellows, "God loves us all, right sure. He loves us all and He giveth and taketh away, He does that." He did not now even remember that Peter was there.

Peter spun around to Ezekiel, his face distorted by passion and fear. "No! No! It will not be my son! It will not be Isaac! The Lord giveth and the Lord taketh away in his own time, when the grain is ripe." He waved his hand as though brandishing a sickle. "When the appointed task is finished. Pharaoh lived eighty-one years, old Wahab eighty-three. I am fifty-nine, and it is not God's wish that my last son should die, that this should be the last generation of my father's name."

"The Lord loves us all," Ezekiel continued, not even looking at Peter, lost in the sonorous rhythm of his own deep, abiding voice. The painting, muddied in spots, was appearing beneath his hands. "The Lord giveth and taketh away."

"No, damn you!" shouted Peter in black frustration at this old fool, this crazy nigger who would not stop chanting and chanting.

"No, I tell you. Isaac will fish in these same waters forty years hence. The Lord will not take him away from me. Rachel will not grieve over the grave of her last flesh. I have built me a tabernacle unto the Lord, and He will hear my prayers. All these long years have not been for nought." Peter stopped, quivering and weak. The old Negro continued chanting. Wahab picked up his tackle which he had dropped on the sand and walked down the beach toward the village.

Behind him, huge black clouds mounted in the northeast, racing precipitously to catch the failing sun. The breakers slapped heavily upon the beach. Ezekiel looked out to sea. "And the Lord Jesus died to save us all," he chanted. "The Lord Jesus died to save us all."

# III

# HOMILETIC

As PETER WAHAB walked down the beach, he was both angry and ashamed. Never before had he allowed himself such luxury; to so shabbily treat poor Ezekiel made him close his eyes in bitter resentment of his own weakness. It was not worthy of him to have acted so poorly. Old Ezekiel didn't understand; perhaps even he, himself, was not fully aware of what had happened these past few weeks.

"God, my own sons," he whispered.

Peter Wahab was a man who had to touch things in order to believe them real. Even his belief in God was a palpable and solid thing to him. God was the islands and the sea, the constant motion of the clouds mounting heavily out to sea and rolling across the Banks. God was Ocracoke and its people—there were no others—and God was the solid, rectangular white church, which Job had helped build so long ago when the Banks were still prosperous.

As he walked along the hard, wet sand, Peter felt the brittle crackle of the small shells one by one. Rachel would already have eaten by now, up from her night's restless sleep. Peter pulled his scarf from his neck up over his nose. The sand was beginning to fly over the beach, and it struck his hands in stinging waves. Rachel would certainly be closing the east and north windows on the cottage. Isaac's room faced the west. The wind wouldn't affect it.

Isaac's room—within which James had died, the little boy with dark, curly hair and brown eyes who when he was only four could swim as well as his father but who had always been afraid of the horses. Peter remembered the day he placed James, squealing in fright and despair (all the while Peter laughing—not knowing), on top of King, the old, placid mount he kept for the family. James screamed and screamed as his father held him firmly upon the unmoving horse. He did not wish to ride, he said, he did not wish to do so. Clear and distinct, his voice had risen above his terror before Peter, in disappointment and frustration, lifted him down while King placidly swished the afternoon flies from his rump. Peter had turned around to find Rachel white, her hands clutching the open barn door, her face contorted and misshapen.

The scene became a painting, an object lesson in some morality that Pharaoh had told him of. King snorted and shifted his feet, but he did so outside the frame. Where were the tall, young men who stood straight as spars before the wind? Why was he himself so earthbound? James ran to Rachel and threw himself into the thick folds of his mother's skirt, hiding his face against her thighs as she sought to comfort him.

Peter had felt cold and deeply lethargic then, as he felt now, walking away from the old ship and turning up the beach through the soft, dry sand next to the low dunes and hillocks of sea oats. He stepped carefully and quickly onto the leeward side of the mounds and began making his way toward the Sound side of the island, walking more easily on the salt meadow and knotgrasses which grew in the island's more protected center. His mother and father had made and sold mattresses of eelgrass that floated in with the tide. Peter could see all the way to the village, although it was still miles away. Little remained of the once great cedar and oak forest of the island; even pines were now rare, and a man generally stood spare and alone above the grasses. The bayberry and goldenrod, even the thick myrtle and yaupon, were stripped by the wind-blown sand until the island's foliage remained flat and level, meekly hugging the ground in a strange harmony of mortification.

Upon reaching the thick shrubbery of the Sound side, Peter turned south toward the village, occasionally swatting a mosquito, still present from the summer's infestation, and watching the Banks ponies as they foraged upon the overgrazed meadows of the island. He passed a beach holly bush, rare upon the Banks, and stopped to break a piece off for Rachel.

Rachel—the homely, sallow-cheeked girl who dressed simply in grays and browns. Not homely really, but plain because of the poverty forced upon her by Jud Payne's bad luck (so everyone said). A right smart girl he had married, industrious and serious, married because Peter had asked her father one morning after church and she had accepted the Sunday next through him.

There had been holly, too, at Christmas when Matthew and Thomas were still alive. It had been hanging there over the doorway while the small, sturdy tree in the living room scented the whole house with its clean, sharp, biting odor. Matthew had not felt well and the family had brought Christmas up to his room, Rachel carrying a tiny sprig of holly, which she held over Matthew's tousled hair as she kissed him. Matthew, straight and true as a cedar. She had pressed him so tightly to her breast that Peter turned his head away, unable to look.

Thomas played his children's games upon the floor.

"Look, look at the fine gentleman jump."

Thomas yelled as he squeezed and let go, squeezed and let go the wooden grips of the toy. Each time the twisted strings would send the little man upon them high above the posts. Around and around he went, over and over again, an absurd circus acrobat in a painted coat and tails. Isaac laughed, too. It was a funny toy, and soon everyone laughed while little Thomas sat on the floor at the side of Matthew's bed and played with his little Christmas toy.

Peter stumbled as he reached the hard-packed sand footpath that ran outside of town and into the pasture. At the road junction, he turned toward Gabriel Midgett's store and proceeded against the wind up the sandy, unpaved street. So Ocracoke was a small town, Peter thought, sleepy and content for two generations. In the days after the Civil War, the railroads had taken all the coastal trade away from the Outer Banks, and Pamlico Sound had eventually proved unsuitable for even lighter traffic from the large ocean ships.

And Johnny Barnes, Peter thought, had died up Hatteras way, almost by accident, in the only act of personal violence upon the islands since King Pharaoh's inexplicable fit of anger. Yes, accident, for surely it was not God's will that a lonely, deaf-and-dumb man should be shot by Yankees merely because he could not hear and they did not know.

The village's dirt roads were those that Pharaoh and Judith had walked along, old Daniel and Bob Howard, the Wahabs and Midgetts and Styrons and Williamses, for generations past. In 1850 the census had found 535 persons living in Ocracoke and 79 families in the village. Fifty years later, there were barely two hundred people. Not only had the outer world failed to remember Ocracoke, but few villagers had remembered the outside world. Young'uns were born in the village, nurtured within the circle of their families, married upon the islands, and provided for by the vocation that had been their fathers'. Few people came to Ocracoke and few people left it. Barter was more common than money, and people wanted for little. Once a month Gabriel's store received stock off the boat down from Hatteras, and Gabriel generally managed to sell enough goods for cash to pay his bills. Thus, when Peter walked up the rickety, gray, weathered steps of the old store, he came to pay his bill, which he did regularly once a month, late or early, and to purchase a length of strong, thick cord on tab for mending some of his nets which were in disrepair due to the hard fall weather.

The store was a place for talking as well as buying, and once within the door, Peter recognized Luke Taylor, one of the Wilson boys, and Herschel Styron. Few men would be out in the Sound this Saturday, what with the weather acting up and all. Gabriel turned from Paul Wilson to Peter across the counter, but the large angular storeowner did not speak.

"My bill, Gabriel, and a measure of cord for the nets. You store-mindin' today?" Peter spoke with the terseness and directness of a man long accustomed to silence.

"Sure thing, Peter. Yes, the missus ailin' a mite. She'll be better tomorrow."

Gabriel went to the register and began leafing through his bills while the other men talked in slow, spasmodic bursts.

"Can't say as I've ever seen such a hard beginnin' to winter."

"Ten year back was a bad'un. Started makin' ice by early November."

"Surf's breakin' the beach down pretty bad off the point."

Peter listened silently. No one expected him to speak, but equally no one knew how to comfort him. Gabriel Midgett was the only intimate Peter had upon the island. It was for him to mitigate his friend's sorrow. For the others, Peter Wahab was a man to respect and admire, even to pity in a fearful way, but he was beyond their help and charity. He chose it so. The room fell into the thin quiet of midmorning, the stillness interrupted only by the wind and the steady creak of the corner rocking chair as Luke Taylor pushed it back and forth, back and forth.

"Yep," said Gabriel as he returned to Peter, "that'll be seven ten, Peter, and here's your cord. Looks like you'll have plenty o' time to be mendin' nets these next days what with this weather comin' in an all—"

"Yep," Herschel Styron interrupted slowly, "I remember two summers back when the beach was bein' hit by a mid-June storm, mommicked to death it was. Well, this here mainlander came in early one mornin', Saturday, like now—and just stared around the store. Remember, Gabe? Looked right bewildered, he did, what with his fancy fishin' clothes on and store-bought flies attached to his cap for decoration. Nothin' sadder than a mainlander lost on the Banks. I didn't know everwhat it was he wanted, so I just waited while he stared and stared.

"Finally he lets the door shut all the way and calls over to Gabriel.

" 'You work here?' he says.

" 'Been known to on occasion,' Gabe says back, quick as a willet.

"Well, you wouldn'ta believed the look on that man's face. Gabe just stood there behind the counter waitin' to do for 'im. Then he clucked a little, like a hen a bit, and went back out the door. Never seen the likes of it. Those folks up north are all alike. Don't know how to talk, they don't. Just can't relax and enjoy the life God gave 'em."

Herschel stopped short, suddenly embarrassed before Peter.

" 'Tis true, Gabriel," Peter quickly responded. " 'Tis true. Aren't many northerners know how to fish or treat folks. Even when I was up north to school those three years Pharaoh sent me, I never made a friend. All too standoffish for me, too cold. They lived by the law up there. A law for this and a rule for that. Couldn't cross the street without looking."

Everyone laughed politely at Wahab's mock anguish. It was a common complaint of Bankers that up north, anyplace off the islands, was too civilized, too rule ridden.

Peter stuffed the cord into his jacket pocket. "No, I'll stay on the islands. They've been good to me all my life, I guess, and I'll stick to 'em like glue yet another spell." He refixed his scarf about his face and walked toward the door. No one offered a goodbye. Luke Taylor continued to rock.

"Day to you, Peter Wahab," Gabriel kindly called out.

"Yep, don't ever remember a summer bad as that'un three years ago," Wilson said. "Usually summers 'round here're pretty mild—"

"Might be, might be," said Luke Taylor, his chair rocking steadily back and forth, "but we're lookin' a bit leeward today."

The door slammed shut behind Wahab as he walked out into the blowing sand and dust.

It took Peter Wahab less than ten minutes to walk from the village store to his home northeast of there, across the creek. He was glad to be gone. Even speaking to his old friends was hard for him nowadays. How much better a friend could one have than Gabriel Midgett, whom he had fished and clammed with all his life, who bought into the old store at a more than generous price when Peter had needed his share pretty badly, who worked with Peter on the church board and was really the only man in town, outside of maybe the minister, now that they had one, who wasn't a bit jealous and put off by Peter's education?

And the lay sermon tomorrow, how would that go? He had given many before, especially when the church had been without a minister for so long, but tomorrow's seemed especially hard. Peter felt dry and used up, and he dreaded the service with all his soul. He turned off the path and into the cottage yard. The palmetto tree, which Pharaoh had planted, swayed under a gust of wind as he opened the door and walked toward the kitchen.

Rachel was busy damping the fire; if a storm was blowing up, no islander would chance that the sparks sucked from his chimney might be cast against his roof. Luke Taylor had lost one house that way, and Rachel was too careful a housewife ever to forget a lesson once learned.

Careful! Peter thought. He must be careful with Rachel.

A careful housewife—and mother, and friend. She had born him children in his old age, even though she feared he might not know how to handle them. But he had loved the children. Loved them all, the resurgence of the "clan," the Wahabs, God's people. The cottage then had reverberated to the incessant din of healthy boys—and the Sound had remained peaceful and quiet, winter-chastened. In the spring they had planted and rebuilt, the snow geese had returned each fall, all untouched by the arrogance of a more civilized world.

"That you, Peter?" she called as the door closed behind him.

"Yes. Took a walk early and been down to Gabriel's for some cord." He deposited his tackle near the door. "I'll be mendin' the nets later on." These days, Peter thought, must remain the same. God will not visit us with so great a burden. "Here's holly for you. I found it on the way home. How's Isaac?"

"About the same, not breathing too easy." Rachel rose and walked toward the cupboard. "But I suspect it'll get better as the day goes. Beth will be over to check him later on. Come get your coffee. Won't be much of a fire before long. Holly, how pretty. Fresh and green as spring itself. Thank you, Peter."

Rachel set a mug of coffee on the kitchen table and kissed her husband as he sat down. Then she went about the kitchen chores that comprised her daily routine. Unlike Peter, Rachel was a woman of habit and order. "A place for everything and everything in its place," she would repeat every time Peter chided her over the undue cleanliness and neatness of their home. But he was secretly proud of her accomplishments, she knew that. Every morning the floors were swept clean of the sand that had accumulated from the day before. Breakfast was fixed, and after the dishes, she would dust downstairs and then go out to the chicken house to check for eggs. If Peter was off early, Rachel even milked the cow before beginning the upstairs cleaning that would occupy her until dinner. Preparing foods for the next day, washing, visiting or shopping, Rachel reserved these for the afternoons; and during the evenings, she would catch up on her mending or possibly read from the large collection of books that Peter had kept since he was a youth but now rarely used.

The routine hardly ever varied day after day, year after year. When Peter would infrequently ask her about it, Rachel would look up at her husband, smile, and say, "I like it this way. It's a good and simple life. I have my boys and husband and the china and knickknacks. Why do you wish it to change, Peter Wahab? Why do you bother me so always?" And she would laugh at him, proud it seemed of her ignorance, of her own stolid refusal to be dissatisfied. Many times Peter had been glad of such a wife. All else is vanity, he thought, but not this.

Rachel finished damping the stove and sat down across the table from him with her own coffee.

> *Two are better than one because they have
> a good reward for their labor.*

(Yes, it was so.) This woman had given him a goodly reward, this flesh of his flesh, heart of his heart, this young girl, now grown old with her love, now thick waisted, with red hands, but still trimly muscled with fine, high breasts; she was his. God had made it so, and He would give them good reward for their labors and suffering.

> *She is like the merchants' ships;
> she bringeth food from afar.
> She looketh well to the ways of
> her household, and eateth not
> the bread of idleness.*

"I don't know how Job Wahab's palmetto tree will make it through another winter," Rachel said. "It's ailin' more and more."

"It'll come back in the summer. Always does."

"But it's such a pitiful thing to see. It's out of place and it suffers. I know it. It's not like the rest of the garden, the myrtles, the yuccas, the azaleas and summer flowers. They were meant to be out here. They close themselves up for the winter and wait for spring, but not that palmetto; and all this time there's nothin' I can do for it."

Her hands moved nervously over the folds of her bodice, straightening and smoothing the coarse muslin.

> *For how can I endure to see the evil
> that shall come unto my people or the
> destruction of my kindred?*

Peter did not know. Her wide, sunburnt face smiled at him from across the table. How unlike the stories Job had told of Judith. He remembered the timidity of their wedding night, his own fumbling and awkwardness. How she had then put her arms around the back of his neck, lifted herself toward him and kissed him, firmly and cooly, and dropped quietly upon the bed again. "Peter," she had whispered, "my Peter." All weakness and timidity had left him then. He had kissed her, and loosening her few remaining petticoats, which he threw in a soft confusion on the floor, he had let his hand fall upon the pink, naked skin, had kissed it and known the intoxication that her body brought him. He had thought it not possible to love a woman as he did that night. He lay until morning with his head near her breasts, feeling the quiet shudder of her breathing and the rhythmic swell of her.

The room was silent.

"The palm will survive, do not worry yourself. I shall tend to the milking," he said finally, finishing his coffee. "You should have seen the shark I almost caught."

"Oh, Peter!"

"I did. I did." He grinned in mock anguish at her unbelief. "And a big one, must have been. A lost white or a blue."

"Peter." Rachel smiled briefly.

"Pulled me near a mile down the beach. Tore the calluses half off my hands and gave me a good dunking. Lucky my arms are still in their sockets, but then I gave him a mite too much slack and lost him. I tell you, he'll take a few lines with him before he leaves these parts, I reckon."

Rachel laughed, sitting straight backed, askance. She laughed so hard that Peter couldn't keep a straight face and he laughed too.

"Oh how you talk, Peter Wahab. You and your sharks. How you talk." Tears ran down Rachel's cheeks.

But he could find nothing more to say. He laughed. Rachel

sniffed and wiped her face with a towel. And the room fell back into silence.

She sat, tired and drawn, facing him, her palms and elbows upon the wooden kitchen table, which he had newly painted only a few months before.

"I've already done the milking, Peter. Don't rush so."

Why had she married him, a man so much older than herself, so slow to understand a woman's needs and passions? Out of fear, the desperate need of a husband, no matter who? He had thought that at first and readily accepted the consequences, but he knew now that Rachel Payne would have died a maid rather than marry a man she did not want. She had done for him too much, born four children too gladly, late in life, tended him too constantly not to love him. She had listened to him year after year as he read the Bible to the children at night. She listened despite the tiny, rapid movements of her hands sewing or knitting in the light of the fire. Rachel never missed a word and would often ask him questions, talking to the boys about the meaning of what her husband had read.

"Doesn't the Preacher in Ecclesiastes only hate this world, Peter, and not the next? If his vanity is so real, he can't possibly know enough even of himself to despair so completely, can he?"

He had tried to explain that hate and rejection were simply not the Preacher's point, but it did no good. Rachel sewed away, her hands moving ceaselessly in complex and rhythmic patterns. She listened carefully, but he could not argue away her lack of understanding.

"The Preacher never heard of Paul's conversion on the Damascus road, Peter. I wonder if he ever felt anything akin to St. John's revelation—which you've never read us in spite of how beautiful it is. Knowing God is a state of mind, a kind of feeling you get. The Preacher didn't know Him, that's all. I think he wished to bargain with God for knowledge instead of believing. The cynic is a man who wishes not to believe because it suits his own vanity, his own hurt pride. No, the world is God's world, Peter, you can be sure of it, and I don't need but my own weakness to know it."

Always that way, he thought. She had taken him in her arms and kissed him that first night and in her weakness made him strong. They had lain naked, flesh against flesh, the firm movement of her hips and stomach underneath him all new and wonderful, all mystery. She had opened herself up to him; and he had come alive for her, breathless in his aching discontent, amazed by his own passion. He had consumed her while her hands, small and frail against him, gripped his shoulders with an urgency he had never dreamed of. Her submission had been perfect in its completeness, and he had received from her a hundredfold. He himself became the debtor, without cause; it seemed, without reason. She had found herself fulfilled, she said, without asking why.

> *I am Alpha and Omega,*
> *the beginning and the end.*
> *I will give unto him that is athirst*
> *of the fountain of the water of life freely.*

"Peter, Peter, I am afraid."

Wahab looked up and saw his wife crying. Her right hand had reached across the table and lay upon his own gnarled fist.

"Peter, he's our last child, and he's no better off now than he was yesterday. The fever's worse—and his breathing is hard. Oh, Peter, he's just like Thomas was, only he's older and he knows what's happenin'. Oh God, Peter, I'm so worn out, so afraid for him."

Peter took his wife's hand in his own. He wished to comfort her, but he did not know how. Why could he not cry also?

Isaac lay upstairs and this woman could do no more. How could he help, and why could he not cry, too, as she did, freely, without shame? Where were the elders now in their wisdom? Why should his son suffer so? Unto what generation of his flesh, which issued out of this woman's body, must this affliction be visited? What had been his transgression?

"Rachel, stop! Stop it, woman!" He heard his voice, imperious. He gripped her hand tightly, and she winced. "It will do no good. No good a-tall. Isaac is a grown boy, older than the others. He has more strength than they. He will get better. He smiles, he sees us. It is not the same. We are a long-lived clan, Rachel. Our men have often wrestled with angels. If Isaac wrestles now, then we must help him. Care for him, tend to the sickness! Keep him covered and warm! Beth will be here before long and she will help. She will help!"

Wahab stood up and walked around the table to his trembling wife. He grasped her by the shoulders and drew her to him. "She's a nurse, Rachel; now quiet yourself. She will know what to do."

"I know, Peter. Elizabeth Turner is a good nurse; but we are so alone on these islands, and she could do so little for the other boys. If Isaac dies, Peter—"

"Hush, it is useless to think about. It is not our decision and it will not happen. God will not leave us alone without a way for our steps. Isaac is a good son. God will not punish us so."

He held her tight and pressed her limp, tired body close to his own. Nothing must hurt this woman. Nothing must hurt her. Not any more. If the world had grown weary, she must not suffer it.

"All things change in God's universe, Rachel. All things change and pass away but this: that I love you, that Issac is a fine and deserving son, and that the Lord will not so unjustly punish us, his servants."

Peter looked out through the window across the tangle of

elder and black locust and bayberry to the Sound. The waters were becoming black and rough. The cordgrass bent itself into the graying sands. Only a few gulls and willets braved the deepening wind now, and even they soon would be gone, bedded down for the storm. Rachel was calm beneath his touch.

"We must go and see to Isaac, Peter."

She shivered.

"It's getting cold enough in the house. We've got to see to it that Isaac's room stays comfortable. I'll get the warmer and a few things. A very small fire upstairs mightn't hurt."

"That's better, that's better. You go about your chores, Rachel, and I'll tend to the boy. We'll spend the afternoon mending nets and reading. I must finish preparing my sermon for the morrow as well. Perhaps Isaac will be well enough by then that you can go with me. Whatever, ask Beth when she comes if she can bide with you awhile during church tomorrow."

ᛯ ᛯ ᛯ

Out on the island's range, old Ezekiel had now left the beach and crossed over to the more protected Sound. The waters were mounting up right hard, they were. No place for an old nigger. He walked quickly along toward the village, scavenging the beach as he went. He was looking for crabs, in particular blue crabs, whose soft and succulent meat might make a fine dinner if he could only find enough. His painting, finished and forgotten, lay on the beach, rising with each wave that found it and floating down the shore. A gust of wind caught it and threw it high in the air. It fell again to the beach, spreading its varied colors upon the sand and then floating further southward as the tide caught it. The wind whined more insistently, and the breakers fell with the sound of cannon against the obdurate, yet ever mutable, sands.

# IV

# THE WARNING

THE DOOR to Isaac's room was hidden at the top of the stairs. The staircase was in an open well and rose directly from the foyer and hall, separating the small cottage into two equal halves. Downstairs, adjacent to the front door on opposite sides of the foyer were a sitting room and a family parlor, which Rachel tried to keep pretty for very special company. Toward the back of the foyer was the spacious kitchen from which Peter had just walked, and across from it a smaller dining room which housed Rachel's china, good linens, and a fine mahogany dining-room set. Upstairs were three bedrooms, one to each side of the stairwell, opening off parallel balconies, and a third room at the head of the stairs, the door of which was swathed in a darkness that the light from the front dormers at the ends of the balconies could not dispel.

Peter stood briefly at the bottom of the steps and stared upward at the obscurely defined doorway. He had to go up there, but he tripped upon the torn sole of his boot and lurched heavily against the bannister, gripping the railing tightly and for a long while remaining motionless. Then, with closed eyes, he pulled himself stiffly erect. All at once, he wanted to hear Isaac laugh again with his little boy's laugh as he ran along the beach, to see the perfect softness of his son's skin next to his shirt, and to feel Isaac's light brown hair against his own rough, unshaven cheek. He had once tried to teach Isaac how to use a fork at the table when he was three years old. He had painfully explained the difference between a fork and a spoon, had explained how to spear meat on the end of the fork, and had finally concluded by telling how long ago men didn't even use spoons and forks at dinner time.

"It was long, long ago, Isaac. Isn't that something?" he had said.

"Yes, Daddy," Isaac had answered. "I knew that."

All the while a sly smile was spreading across the boy's face as he looked at his father, who turned to see Rachel laughing to herself and even young James in his high chair looking quickly from face to face, burbling happily, babylike, as the entire table began to laugh in unison. Even at three, Isaac often did such things to his father, letting Peter labor over explanations that the boy was able to understand very easily.

He had always been a quick boy, to understand, to laugh, to love, and to enjoy other people. Peter mounted the stairs slowly and silently, his legs heavy, his hands manacled to the bannister.

The disease was not pretty or easy, and that certain knowledge made Peter's visitation much worse. Isaac could laugh no more. His wasted, febrile body lay behind the door upon a bed Peter knew would be damp with his son's sweat. It had happened this way with all four children. At first, there had been merely the sore throat and coughing, which neither Peter nor Rachel had taken too seriously. They had put each child to bed and taken the normal precautions against possible bad colds. Nothing, however, had worked. The onions and sugar, which Rachel boiled into a rich, thick, tangy syrup, had done no good at all, not even the kerosene and sugar, which Peter had insisted upon trying this time (over Rachel's repeated objections). A tablespoon of sugar and four drops of kerosene; he had never known it not to help a cough or fever, and yet Isaac became worse. True, Beth Turner often laughed at such remedies, but nothing that she prescribed seemed to help. Isaac's fever worsened; he had refused to eat for days now. His voice had become hoarse of late, and in these last few days his breathing was labored and irregular. Isaac's throat was sticky and gray, with a large cottony membrane forming along the top and back of his mouth. It had happened like this with the others as well, but Beth had not seemed as concerned about it in those cases. Actually, no one had paid much attention to the membrane. Now Beth seemed worried, and as Peter opened the door to Isaac's room he dreaded her return almost as much as he prayed for it. His son must not die! He would not let himself believe that possible. Isaac's body lay upon the bed, small and inert. Only the ever-restless head and the hollow wheezing of his son's lungs reassured him. The boy was still alive.

Peter stepped gently across the room and tended to the small fireplace near which Isaac's bed was placed. He then checked for drafts around the two windows which looked out upon the backyard and garden, felt carefully along the mouldings, and finally sat quietly upon the chair next to his son's bed. He bent over, ran his hand lightly over the spread, smoothing out the wrinkles and folds of Isaac's anguished sleep. Then he leaned back in the chair, glancing anxiously as Isaac moved fretfully under the covers. He remained silent and unmoving for a few minutes, continuing to stare at his son's worn, thin face. Peter was still and lethargic as if dead himself, his lips wet with saliva that he had neglected to swallow, until the fire hissed sharply and one of the new logs he had put upon it fell forward into the screen. As he crossed beyond the bed and lifted the screen away, Peter did not hasten to fix the damage but remained dumb and motionless before the smoldering log.

✦ ✦ ✦

"Now it gettin' little and little— Hey, something made it ts-ts, I hear it go."
It was on a late Saturday afternoon in warm summer.
"Hey, Mom, what are you making—it's stop and go, stop and go. Did you know that, br-ts-ts, brr-ts-ts?"
The day lengthened into the hidden softness of evening and Isaac played on. Empty whelks and cowries lay in his sandbox beside the screened back porch, where Rachel sat, passive and content, beginning to sew. Her long, thick skirt rustled as she crossed her legs. A coot flew north along the Sound's edge. The sun was still two hours from setting across the Pamlico, but already, deep red and purple bruised the once blue horizon. There was nothing more beautiful than sunset—its colors searing the sky, vast and tremulous. One could actually see God's will in movement, close and palpable, the whole

world throbbing to that one tremendous heartbeat. It was lay-by time in August, a period of comparative idleness and enforced relaxation. The fish had stopped running. Big trap nets lay drying along the Sound or in backyards, waiting to be mended. Each day the currents washed up and down the shore hundreds of jellyfish, their soft, liquid putrescence corrupting the sands for weeks. The last few crops in the gardens had been planted, the horses turned to pasture. The air was redolent with the pungent smells of the fall harvest.

"Hey you, stay there." Isaac ran on awkward, chubby legs across the yard. "Hey, got so little, ts-ts, look it. One horse out of the barn. Giddap horse, I can't see you. Trees are made of animals." Momentarily dejected, Isaac returned to the sandbox, picked up a bright auger, and began to dig with it. The thin shell snapped and he began to cry. Rachel laughed. .

"Some things must be handled carefully, Isaac. Augers are too small and fragile to be handled so roughly. Dig with the scallops or clam shells, but never the augers or a wentle. They're much too rare and beautiful."

Peter sat and watched—and listened. He was repairing his nets—one in particular that had to be mended in several places. All the work would not be finished until the Monday next, and so he was leisurely and slow about his actions.

Then they all heard it, there under the dying, furnacelike sun. It was a thin, high scream, its pitch so tinsel and pure it almost hurt his ears. It seemed to come from nowhere, and yet the sound invaded every corner of the yard, closing in upon him, shrieking not louder but more intense, more in terror as second by second it became higher and higher, its thin threadlike intensity never wavering. Peter looked from Isaac to Rachel and perceived their blank directionless stares. The world contracted, became only the small backyard within the circumference of the continuing, shrill whistle.

He caught a quick movement to his left. Something had dropped from the thick protecting branches of the live oak and now lay upon its back in the sandy earth, squirming awkwardly to and fro. All the while emanating from it was the terrified whistle, unending and unchanging. It was a large, gray, pupalike cicada, fat, curvilinear, and helpless upon the ground. On top of it was an adult digger wasp, its black, powerful appendages holding fast to the soft, pustulelike thing squirming beneath it. The wasp was stinging the cicada. Again and again and again, it seemed. Nothing else in the yard moved. The wasp remained mortally fastened to the soft, white stomach of the cicada as the high, thin whirring filled the yard. Louder and louder. Peter stared helplessly at the carnality before him. The whir broadened to a tremolo. He was aware only of it, of nothing else than its aching hollowness.

Then it stopped. The whistling stopped. The large, black wasp lazily withdrew itself from the inert cicada and flew calmly away toward the bushes beyond the yard.

The world grew large again. Isaac was sucking his thumb. Rachel was whimpering in a soft choke. The sun was sharply outlined in the darkening sky. A breeze rustled through the limp bushes that bordered the yard. Peter realized that he was shaking violently, still clutching with whitened knuckles the portion of fishnet in his hand. The wasp would be back, Peter knew, to gather up the still-living offal, to bury it alive so the wasp's young could feed on its still-warm, sweet flesh. And the cicada would endure a living death until, only toward the very end, a major organ would be eaten and the cicada would die.

⁊ ⁊ ⁊

The fire snapped and Peter wakened. He felt sweat upon his face and quickly took tongs to lift the log back upon the grate. He replaced the small, black screen, stood up, and wiped his face with a handkerchief which he pulled from his back pocket. The floor creaked as he walked back to Isaac's bedside and sat down. Shriveled, inert, and alone, Isaac lay upon the bed, not staring now, not small, not wide eyed and bewildered, but hot and rigid in his sleep. A picture of him on his first birthday hung directly above the bed and above it a smaller picture of Isaac in a white, lace-edged christening gown. It was the same gown Job had been christened in, and Peter himself, and every Wahab, James and Matthew, and Thomas, even Judith, who had so long ago deserted the islands leaving only a short note which her father had read and burned. All had been christened in that same gown. It never changed.

Peter looked up as the door opened and Rachel carefully, almost timidly, he thought, entered the room. She brought moistened towels for Isaac's head, and after closing the door behind her, quickly crossed the room, sat opposite her husband, and looked for a long while at the sleeping boy.

"He seems better, Rachel," Peter said. "He hasn't been as restless the last half hour, and his breathing seems a mite easier."

Rachel looked up, and for a second, the pause recorded only in the minute falter of her head as it turned from the boy, she stared at her husband. The lines in her face were accentuated by the dimness of the room and the fire behind her. The folds of her long skirt crumpled upon the floor beneath her chair, and the straight line of her back, her fine carriage, made Peter think that he had never seen her so beautiful, so very much a woman. Then the windows rattled as a gust of wind caught them, and she looked away.

" 'Bout the same, I guess," she said. "Don't imagine we'll really see a change till Beth arrives. Maybe she's got some good news from the doctor at Beaufort— My poor boy, so small, so sick, and so very good."

Rachel moved to the window. "What can we do for him, Peter? What can we do? He hasn't woken up yet since last night. I'm afraid for him, so very afraid."

She stopped, continued to look out the window, and smoothed her hair back from her face. She turned and moved back to Peter, steadying herself on the back of his chair. "It hasn't been a good year for the rest of the village either. So many folks sickly, the Farrows' children and Tom Aul's young'uns. It's not natural for so much sickness to be about. Lord knows we've all so many heartaches, but I just don't know what to do. Gabriel's out of British oil. I thought I might try some on sugar for Isaac's cough."

She went to the bed, leaned over Isaac, and changed the compress that lay upon his forehead, immersing a used towel in the basin next to her, wringing it out, and refolding it for use again. For a long time neither of them spoke. The quiet hardened within the room, became rigid and stiff in an awful silence of unforgiving, its adamantine surface broken only by a drip of water from Rachel's towel and the suffused glow of occasional afternoon light that capriciously penetrated the shaded windows. Shadows began to haunt the corners and crevices.

Then, as if again from a dream, Peter awoke to the soft pressure of his wife's hand upon his shoulder. "Come, Peter," she said. "There is nothing we can do. It's late. Come, you've had little to eat all day, and we cannot have you sick too. The storm's building. You must see to the yard and stock."

The storm was building up, but Peter hadn't realized it. He hadn't heard. As he got up from the chair and followed his wife out of Isaac's room, he tried to remember what he had just been thinking of, and he could not. What had made the time so short (and faceless)? Was he thinking of Judith, of the time when Job told him long ago he heard Judith was dying up north and he would not go to see her, his own daughter and blood? Peter couldn't remember. And it frightened him even more.

He reached the bottom of the stairs and saw hanging on the left of the doorway Rachel's Sevres plate. How long ago was it she had gotten that plate? Had he given it to her shortly after their marriage when he had made one of his infrequent trips up to Nags Head and Manteo to buy feed for the horses after the hard winter of '86—or '79? Or had Job given it to her, along with all those other presents he had so carefully packed up in a large wooden box shortly before he died (as if he had known—it seemed) and told Peter to save for his own wife, if he was ever to marry late. Peter never opened that box. He gave it to Rachel on their wedding day as Job's gift, as Pharaoh would have wanted it, he was sure. How surprised she was then, and happy, too. It was as if all the wide, outside world had suddenly descended upon the little cottage to which he brought her. He watched as Rachel picked out the things one by one, each more strangely exotic than the last.

A tablecloth and twelve napkins. "All Irish linen, Peter. Imagine, Irish linen, here. Oh, Job must have been a very rich man."

Then there were rings and brooches, too, even a small, delicate gold ring for a child, with a deep black onyx in the middle. There was a whole set of Royal Grafton bone china decorated with fine and intricate edgework, medieval in its reasoned complexity. Like the Lindesfarne Gospels, he had thought, remembering too the story from some book he had read long ago about St. Cuthbert. At the center of each piece were three large birds perched upon the final, thin limbs of an unseen tree. Each had a great red crest and an immense, long red tail, spotted black and yellow. Their wings were banded red, yellow, and green while with their long, pointed black beaks and deep, sinuous ruby throats, they seemed to vie for authority and dominion—there in the inside of the cup. Placed carefully upon the table, they always made the dining room seem a world apart—as did the other dish, the Chinese dish, all gold and ivory, so thin you could not only see through it but see things up to six feet away through its fragile porcelain. Rachel had put that dish upon the dining-room wall, and its strange, artless gaggle of monks with large eyes, scraggly beards, and threadbare robes looked out upon each Sunday dinner, year after year.

But where did this plate come from, upon the foyer wall, and what had he been thinking of up there in the room? There was Limoges china, too, in that great box, a huge water pitcher with delicate pink flowers rising from long, green stalks. Like a psalmody, a psalmody it was, to see Rachel so happy, so excited, the melody intoned upon her face in the lines of her mouth and cheek, the way her chin reached upward as she laughed. The riches of the world were before them. Job had left all this—a heritage to an unknown woman who would bear the next generation of his family. Had it been Jenny Payne's? Surely Pharaoh would not have left just "any" gifts. Why these things? Of what great importance were they? What kind of riches could be left by one man to his son, for surely that's what he was—the son of Job Wahab as certainly as if he had been born so?

Rachel called from the kitchen and Peter left the little dish. He went into the parlor and sat down heavily upon the sofa.

"I'll bring you a bit in a minute, Peter. We can set a spell and talk."

That was not like Rachel. The kitchen was for eating, special occasions and Sundays belonged to the dining room, but they rarely snacked in the parlor, with its neatly starched doilies, thick carpet, and fragile knickknacks. Little ever changed in this room; it remained forever beautiful and cool. The long green velvet drapes (Job's gift, too) confined the room in a diffidence of shadow and darkness. The patterned wallpaper was his father's, put up years ago, still clean in its faded silhouettes. Peter looked around. He had never bought or made one piece of furniture for this room.

Rachel entered on noiseless feet and placed a tray of coffee and small, trimmed sandwiches upon the low table in front of him. She walked around the table and sat down next to him.

"Roaches are gettin' bad in the kitchen, Peter. I'll have to clean them out soon again, if you'll help move the heavy furniture for me. I had to trim the crusts off all of one loaf. That room needs a good cleanin' out. The sandwiches look nice, though, don't they? Sort of special, like something festive was going to happen."

As if this loveliness could go on forever, and forever, and forever.

"I saw you looking at the dish in the hallway. Pretty, isn't it?" Rachel, now a journey away from him across the sofa, was molded and in low relief against the repetitions of the wallpaper, friezelike, talking slowly in quiet, nervous spurts.

"Mother bought me that many years ago. Don't know if I ever told you. She was up at Elizabeth City staying with a relative of ours who was dying. She'd kept watch most all of the day; in fact she'd been there well into three weeks, us young'uns alone, home with Pa and all, and my aunt just lying in bed, not able to move and sickly so that she didn't even want to talk, just lying there, holding tight to Mother's hand. Well, Mom couldn't take any more of it. She took the little money she had and went into town right after she left her sister, and she spent it all. It must have been like a holiday. Mom said she couldn't get over the feeling that it was, buying things like she'd never done before in her life, a new dress shirt for Pa, white fancy gloves for Jane, Lord, I don't remember what else. And that plate for me, all the way from

Europe. Not so practical, she didn't buy one thing we could use, 'cept on special occasions. She even bought some animal crackers for little Billy. A week later we all had some when she brought them home, and Billy went around the room givin' each of us one cracker, all strange animals we'd never seen, lions and elephants, hippopotamuses and the like. And we sat there next to the fire eating them while Pa growled about how we'd all go naked that winter because of Mom's foolishness. 'All go bare' is what he said, and me not carin' a bit, just holdin' that plate so close to me I almost lost my breath and thinkin' I'd never seen anything so beautiful before."

> *For the flesh lusteth against the Spirit; and the Spirit against the flesh, but the fruit of these is love.*

Love, he was thinking of love up in the room.

"Silly, isn't it, Peter, how those things stay with a body forever?"

Rachel picked up a small sandwich and bit into it. The hot coffee was steaming in the chilly room. Automatically his hand raised the cup to his mouth. The window rattled violently and then stopped. The wind moaned coarsely about the house. He wondered how many birds were still flying.

"How do we care for each other, I wonder? Mom there, loving her sister so much, and yet she said she felt it was like a holiday or such, buyin' those presents for us."

> *Who is a rich man? He that is content with his portion. When thou eatest the labor of thy hands happy shalt thou be and it shall be well with thee.*

There was a loud knocking at the door, which mixed with the urgency of the wind. "Oh, that must be Beth. Thank God she's here." Rachel got up and crossed toward the door, the anxious lines on her face losing some of their tension and rigidity.

✓ ✓ ✓

*I shall but love thee better* ....

He remembered Amy Harris, far up the islands, who had never learned to swim and who had been saved from drowning by big John, her husband, one day when their fishing dinghy sprung a leak out in the Sound. John had swum a mile and a half to shore with Amy clinging to his back, and Amy had never forgotten it. She had vowed to repay him in kind.

Then, a few years back, shortly after Amy died, a hurricane, the second of that year, had headed toward the Banks. Most everyone had evacuated the village, but John had stubbornly refused to go inland. His Amy was there, out back, and he was going to stay with her.

The hurricane was a bad one. It cut half a dozen new inlets along the Banks, swept across almost all the outer islands. Villages all along the Banks were hurt terribly by the water (although inexplicably he found his own house largely unharmed when he and Rachel and the boys returned to it from Manteo, where they had gone for protection).

John Harris had remained near the large cement vault in which he had placed Amy's body until the power of the wind made breathing so difficult that he had been forced inside the house. Then, about midnight, the house started to break up, windows crashing to the floor, doors springing open and wrenching from their hinges, the water, knee-deep inside the house, tearing at the supports. John had struggled to the front door just as the south side of the house stove in only to see Amy's vault, driven by the wind, pounding against the foundations of the house, which collapsed in a welter of wood, studs, and sea. John flung himself atop the vault and prayed for his own life, at that moment more animal than man. They found him two days later, still clinging to the vault, some thirty miles across the Sound under some cypress trees at Sandy Point. He was alive. A miracle, most felt.

> *I shall but love thee better . . . .*
> *In the fulness of time . . .*
> *to be redeemed under the law.*
> *And Abraham had two sons.*

✶ ✶ ✶

"Peter, Peter, Beth's here. Look up! Where on earth are you, Peter Wahab?"

It was Rachel's voice, and he started up from the sofa to see the broad, kind face of Elizabeth Turner smiling down at him from the middle of the room.

"Afternoon, Peter." Beth's long, heavy wool skirt was moist and clung heavily about her legs. Her face was long and drawn. The trip back from Beaufort must have been a hard one, Peter thought. It was a good twenty-five or more miles up to Atlantic from Beaufort, most of it through low, mosquito-infested swampland, with few people and fewer towns along the way. Sealevel and Atlantic, but there couldn't be more than a hundred souls in either of those. Then came the lonely boat ride along the Core Banks to Ocracoke. A good thirty miles up the Sound and today in a mean sea as well. It must have been a hard trip, and yet Beth was here, not even out of her traveling clothes, all out of breath, not from running but from the force of her own emotion. Peter made to rise.

"No, no, Peter, don't get up. Let me just sit a spell."

"I'll go get a cup of coffee, Beth," Rachel said, smoothing her hair. "You and Peter sit and gossip. Isaac's still asleep."

Both of them watched Rachel leave the room. Beth seated herself carefully across from Peter and smiled politely. It was not like her. There was almost pity in her manner, in the broken surfaces of her face as she spoke to him about the ride over on the boat and the bad weather. She was waiting for Rachel to return. What had Beth found out from the doctor at Beaufort? He wanted to know, but he would not ask. She would tell him in God's own good time, and Peter grimly set his mouth against it.

Rachel entered with a steaming cup of coffee. The good china, Peter noticed. There would be an empty spot in the dining-room cabinet where she had removed it. She gave the cup to Beth and then resumed her seat next to Peter. Beth took a sip, fretfully put the cup down on the table next to her, and looked across the room at the two of them.

"Peter, Rachel, I've something to tell you. Now, I don't want you to get upset. It's not all that bad, but it—well, it isn't good either. I'm pretty sure now that what Isaac has is diphtheria."

Rachel caught her breath but said nothing. Peter looked slowly around the room and then stared silently at Beth.

"Now, calm yourselves some. Isaac is an older boy and a strong one. There's every hope he'll make it through. It's just that we've always been pretty healthy out here on the islands, and what with me not having a great deal of training and all, I wasn't sure I recognized it until a few days ago. Even then I kept thinking it might just be a bad fever or such and . . . ."

Beth stopped and put her face down into her hands. She didn't cry, but her voice broke as she talked.

"Oh, Peter, Rachel, I'm so sorry. I just didn't know. It's

the same thing that took the other boys, and I didn't see it. I didn't see it. I wasn't looking for it what with all our other problems this year. It's a common enough sickness on the mainland. There's a white membrane that forms in the back of the mouth that's a sure sign. Children are extremely susceptible. With James and Matthew, I just plain didn't see it. I thought for sure it was pneumonia, and the doctor said that's eventually what takes many of them. The poison gets in the bloodstream and affects the heart, and the lungs fill up. We've had such a bad year, so much malaria this summer and fall, and so much croup and pneumonia this winter, I just . . . ."

Rachel rose and placed her hand on Beth's shoulder. "Oh Beth, Beth, you done all you could. We know that. Now don't fret so," she crooned abstractedly, staring at the carpet.

"We did, Rachel, we really did, even though I didn't know it at the time. There's no cure or medicine for it, but over half the cases get better." Beth was talking quickly. "There's every hope for Isaac. There really is. With little Thomas, I saw that white membrane, but I just couldn't remember what it was. He went so fast that by the time I found it in my books it was too late. And then with Isaac I had to see the doctor in Beaufort to be sure. Isaac's already lived longer than usual. He might reach a crisis and start getting better any time now. We've got to keep him warm and make it as easy as possible for him to breathe. I'm sure it'll work out. The Lord won't let you lose another one like this. We'll work hard at it."

Peter rose slowly. He felt infinitely tired and wanted to close his eyes, but he didn't. "Come, Beth, let's go upstairs. You've been a great help to us and a great comfort to Rachel in these times, and what you say is right true. The Lord won't."

But even as they walked up the stairs once more, Peter lowered his eyes and could not look at the black, shrouded doorway. At the end, he could not walk up those stairs at all, and he waited in the sitting room while Rachel and Beth went in to see his son. He winced at the sharp click of the door as it opened, and he strained to hear the labored and hollow breathing that he knew must be Isaac's. The boy was not any better. Beth must stay the night with Rachel. He would ask her that. He listened as the women talked in low whispers. Isaac was still not awake, perhaps in a coma now. Maybe the crisis would come this night and tomorrow would find Isaac better and awake, smiling and laughing at them for all their worry. Yes, that might very well happen, and he would give God thanks as never before for his son's safe passage through.

Peter opened the front of the secretary. He would finish his sermon. It was getting on toward suppertime, and the minister had promised to pay a call. As he picked the papers out of the desk, he thought a bell was ringing over and over in the storm. He listened again. Nothing, only the cold screech of the wind. No, he must have been mistaken. One couldn't hear a ship's bell from all the way across the island, not in this wind. Still, he was on the north side of the house. No, only the howl of the wind, which would get worse ere the morrow. Peter walked to his chair, sat down, and began preparing his notes for the morning.

# V

# VISITATION

IT WAS NICE of Beth to offer to stay, Rachel thought, as she prepared supper that evening. Nice, especially since the poor thing hadn't even been home after her journey and all. She really shouldn't have let her, yet with Isaac still so bad— Oh God, if he ever died, what would she do, and Peter acting so tired and afraid? Well, she needed the help and that was that! She was too tired herself to do so much alone, what with the minister coming and a good supper needed for him.

Peter worried her. He wasn't right, too sullen and angry. She had never seen him like this and had never expected, no matter what befell them, to see him so. That was bad, when he hadn't got up for Beth when she entered the room. Peter was one of the most educated men in the village, a gentleman right through. She'd never seen anything that had made Peter forget to be kind and mannerly.

Rachel stirred the blackened pot on the fireplace and tested the strong, thick broth. She then crossed to the table and began breading the oily, white drum fillets, which were to be served when the minister arrived. She thought of Peter in the sitting room working on his sermon. Why, even Reverend Hawkins was not able to speak with the beauty and awfulness of her Peter. He was a rock of the church, as everyone knew. And yet this. She had heard stories about how her husband had given up old Pharaoh's fortune, all that the Wahabs had built during their years upon the Banks. Peter was a good and godly man. He'd always looked after the boys well—sometimes, she thought, too well. He'd been too loving—too fiercely possessive of them and proud. He'd taught all four the ways of the islands and the sea. Perhaps that was the trouble. Lord knew it was a lonely and hard life, but there were rewards. There were people and friends. Still, Peter always seemed to have so few, only Gabriel and old Ezekiel, such as he was. And even Gabriel seemed more Peter's friend by design than by desire. Peter was never much of a social talker. Even with the boys, he taught more by example and the deep well of love that lay at the bottom of his silence.

Maybe that was why old Ezekiel made such a good companion for him. Zeke would say nothing and just fish, the two or them sitting there in the inlet for hours, deep in the morning rhythm of their lives, never touching or talking but feeling only the powerful, dragging monotony of the waves and current. There was always something unrepentant about Peter. He was at times too predictable, too positively reasonable and knowing. Like giving up his family's wealth—he was always so sure about it, so confident that he was right. She'd often thought that Peter could never have been that way if he'd been poor to begin with, had really known what it was like to have nothing and to have to make do.

She reproached herself fiercely. Didn't she enjoy and appreciate all he had given her? Certainly they had never gone hungry, and the house was as snug and fine a home as the village had, right on the creek side, protected by yaupon and cedar and live oak. Quite a difference from the windy, cold, point-side home she'd come from.

And Peter had not given up everything. In spite of what he said and might like to think, he'd been a mite too practical for that. He'd kept the old treasure box from Job, which he gave her on their wedding day, always saying he never knew there were things in it like that. He'd kept a goodly sum of money, too, in the bottom drawer of the great rosewood chest in their bedroom. How much she didn't know, for she'd never counted it in spite of all the times she'd wanted to. Peter had never hid the money. It didn't matter that much, he'd always protested, yet it was always there whenever they needed a little extra. There, just like all the beautiful and expensive furniture was there, which old Wahab had bought for Hosea so long ago and to which Pharaoh had added so diligently over the years.

Her husband, Rachel decided, had never really been a happy man. In their early years together she would often ask him about it, hurt by his overseriousness, the almost petulant sense of his despair. He'd always laughed and said, "Don't worry, woman. God is complete in grief as well as in joy."

That was all. She'd accepted that. She had to. There was nothing else to do, and Peter with his learning could always get around her. Besides, with the boys coming along, it hadn't been as noticeable any more, what with diapers and two-o'clock feedings and the loss of personal intimacy that inevitably came with the babies. Not that she regretted it, not at all. Peter was a good father, the best on the islands; but somehow they had grown apart, and now, when they needed each other so much, he was like this, so distracted and drawn in. What was she to do?

Rachel finished breading and set the fish on a table near the sink. She stirred the pot carefully and swung it back from the fireplace a little to let it simmer. Perhaps some tea before dinner when he arrived or a small glass of wine—Minister Hawkins wouldn't mind. He knew his Bankers by now, and surely he knew Peter. Yes, wine would be acceptable. She went into the dining room and removed from the cabinet the delicately etched decanter and four of the six small glasses that were situated on the lower of three glassed shelves. She carried them into the living room and set them down on the table; then she called Peter to get the Concord wine for her in order to fill up the decanter.

"Have you finished your sermon, Peter?" she said as he entered the room. "I was a bit afraid of botherin' you, but I can't get those corks out of the bottles. Never could."

"For the little wine we drink, you've no need to, now have you?" Peter seemed a bit more relaxed as he spoke. Maybe it was better now with Beth here and the minister coming.

"No, that's true enough, but I do need you, husband. Minister Hawkins will be here soon, and I've yet to set the table and all. Come in with me and take down the china while I spread the linen."

Peter looked up from his work with the cork and bottle. How foolish she was, how delightfully foolish. She didn't really need him in the other room, and his sermon was just nearing completion. If he just worked hard for ten or fifteen minutes— Such stuff from Rachel. Surely she could get along without him right now. Most anyone could handle the dishes —certainly for only four people.

Rachel was still a strong, fine figure of a woman. He stared absently at her for a moment. How carefully the growing shadows imprisoned the folds of her dress. He had not lately noticed how deep and distinct the lines had become in his wife's face. She was a beautiful woman, though, in spite of it all, perhaps more beautiful now in her sadness than she had been as a little girl, a slip of a girl, so long ago when he first saw her, years before they were married, before he'd asked old Jud for her. The asking then was made only to formally seal the unspoken bond already made so many times before by him, of which no one knew but he himself was so positive, so sure that this quiet, lonely girl was to be his. More beautiful now even—but the hall and window lamps would have to be lit—Rachel's face became hidden in the shadows of the room—and he must finish his sermon. He pulled hard on the cork and abruptly it popped free. He lurched backward slightly, and a little wine trickled down the side of the bottle.

"One thing at a time, wife, one thing at a time. I almost spilled the wine what with your talking. I'll light the hall lamps while you set dinner. I'd only be in the way with my ten thumbs. Perhaps, too, I can finish the sermon if I hurry."

Rachel winced. He was trying to get away. She knew so even if he did not. She wanted to talk with him. She must! She wanted to rediscover with him their lost children who were not, could not be, truly ever lost if she had borne them and suckled them. They would not be lost if she could but remember them within the now-quiet house. But this man would not let her have her children any more. Now when she needed him so much, he would not come to her, and she grew afraid, not of the inevitability of Isaac's death—if that was to be—but of the increasingly grim and immobile face that often seemed no longer to need or want her.

"No, Peter! Come help me. The dishes are too high and too heavy. I'm tired, what with fixin' dinner and all, and if you let things sit a spell, the sermon will come."

Peter smiled thinly. He was nervous and he feared that she saw it. "The lamps, girl, the lamps. Would you have Minister Hawkins stumble into a coal black house? Now go about your chores and I'll be with you in a few minutes."

"Peter, please!" Rachel was desperate. He would not leave her, not now! She would not let him. Not now. "Peter, I need your help. I can't do it all alone. Oh, please."

"Rachel, Rachel!" Peter quickly grabbed his wife, who had begun to cry, and disarmed by her, he had no words of comfort. He was afraid and confused by her weakness. "Stop it. Stop it." He intoned the words over and over, holding her next to him for a long time.

Then suddenly, she pushed away from him, wiping her eyes with the lace cuff of her dress and brushing stray hair back along her head.

"No, Peter. No! Not this time. You must talk with me. It's been weeks, months, since we've talked. Always so closed up, so tight and drawn away."

She held her chin high and continued to cry as she spoke. Peter wanted to help her, to hold her again, but he didn't know how. Then he wanted to leave, to get away from her, to close his eyes and hear only the sea and see the strange patterns sunlight made upon it on a clear June day.

"Peter, speak!" Rachel screamed at him. "Damn you, Peter Wahab, speak."

And then she was hitting him in the face and chest with pitifully ineffectual blows from her small, awkward hands. Peter tried to grasp her hands, but he could not, and finally smothered her blows by hugging her tightly to him. Rachel gasped as he took her breath away. She became limp in his embrace, crying heavily against his chest.

"Stop it," he said sternly. Peter held his wife tightly with one hand and slapped her hard across the face with the other. "Stop it, Rachel! Have you lost your sense, woman? All this over the setting of a table? This is not the time nor the place for such actions." Rachel was still sobbing, but she stood alone and stared dully at the floor.

"I didn't know you to be so tired. I'm sorry for that. You must get a good night's rest after dinner. We'll send Marcus home early, and Beth and I will stay up with Isaac. I can work on my sermon then. Now take hold of yourself and go put the linen on the table. I'll light the lamp near the window and be in to help with the dishes."

Rachel obeyed meekly. This was the first time Peter had ever hit her, and together with her own panic, the blow created within her a profound lassitude. She stopped crying. Then she did as he bid her. She had failed, and now only the urgency of dinner remained. Soon, she must get dinner.

"I'm sorry, Peter. I was tired and— Oh God . . . . It shan't happen again."

"Don't, Rachel, don't!" was all that Peter replied, and he turned away. He felt sorry for this woman who needed him so. He wanted to help her, to hold her and comfort her, but he could not. "I'm sorry, too . . . that I hit you. I didn't mean to hurt."

"I know," she said and left the room.

Peter lit the black wick of the oil lamp and followed his wife into the dining room. They set the table impassively, taking down from the cupboard the heavy ivory and gold-leafed plates and the more delicate cups and saucers with the gold pattern repeating itself, in silent, perfect harmony, again and again around the edges. They had just completed the settings when Minister Hawkins's loud knock announced him. Peter assured himself of the table's order before he followed his wife into the foyer.

Minister Marcus Hawkins was not a large man; rather he was tall and lank with a gait that would have seemed awkward and even rambling if it had not been informed and disciplined by his superior education. He was here to see Peter about the lay service of the following morning and to pay a customary sick call upon the family.

He was relatively new to the Banks. He had been appointed some twenty years before to serve and minister to the islanders shortly after the church had split into two groups. The more liberal "northern" families, who allowed dancing and drinking (in moderation), had built their own church, a simple, square, whitewashed building on the south side of town. It had often been whispered that Minister Hawkins, down from up north and so obviously cultured with his learning and city ways, really sympathized with the dissenters, but nothing came of it. Peter had taken to him right away, and that alone carried a great deal of weight with the other parishioners. Marcus Hawkins, thus, judiciously waited out the period of his discomfiture.

He seldom acted on his own authority, nor did he ever fail to act on the word of others. He understood very well that his flock was neither spiritually liberal nor deeply conservative. The reformed church, a third group in town, which had also split from the original Methodist congregation, attested to that. Better to wait, and all things possible in this little community would be his.

He worked diligently and hard, if without fervor. His lack of spiritual ecstasy wasn't missed because the congregation left to him didn't want it. Actually, Mr. Hawkins was the perfect preacher, they thought. He saw babies into the world and old men out of it. He preached his sermons directly from the Bible in the homilies that he had quickly learned the Bankers appreciated. During his first ten years on the Banks he did not marry, and it wasn't till women started talking about how nice it would be to have a minister's wife again to help reorganize the Daughters of Mary that he did marry. Then his wife was very naturally an island girl—Rebecca Styron, Herschel's youngest and prettiest daughter.

It was a match universally approved of, and Marcus had settled down to a large and influential life within the community. If he ever felt pinched and cheated at his loss of a greater and more commodious society in Virginia, Marcus Hawkins never openly showed his disappointment. He was by nature a man given to reflection and contemplation. A lesser age might have seen him as slothful; a greater, as regenerate. What was more, if the minister actually did live under such sin, he was perfectly capable of the many rationalizations necessary in order to suffer in good grace. A fine and more remunerative parish would have required more work, more condescension to the richer parishioners, more study, and constant communication with church authorities. In short, more responsibilities and more duties. It would have been nice, but the rewards were not worth the effort, especially when one could have relatively so much upon the islands.

It was his "station" that mattered most to Marcus Hawkins, and within the isolated village of Ocracoke he was a supreme authority. He even congratulated himself that one could save much more money there and live much more cheaply within a superior standard of living than anywhere else in the country. Every three months he would travel to Manteo to see his brother churchmen of the Conference and to put in the town's one bank, at interest, the larger portion of his salary. He thus gained a reputation as a strict and godly man.

And he was careful as well to enlarge his dominion. As

minister of the oldest of the village's churches, Marcus Hawkins knew that he had about him by right the mystique of ancient authority. He was, therefore, careful not to misuse it. He knew how to preach about a God of grace and love. He could discover the righteousness of even the blackest sinner, and often he could be heard remarking on how all God's children must live together in peace and love. Essentially, that had been what all the Ocracokers did before Hawkins arrived, but he was the first to articulate such an ecumenical spirit clearly.

Even the two schisms that had occured over the last one hundred years were largely the result of habit, more than belief or revelation. "The younger folks just naturally wanted to wander a little each generation," Ed Manners had once said, and the good minister was quick to seize the wisdom of the remark. He found Peter Wahab to be the most intense spiritual force in the community and one of the village's most respected members. Surprisingly, too, Peter's religious perception seemed to interlock easily with his own rather formal vision of the inseparable Christian community bound in love of God and devotion to his word.

He, therefore, cultivated Peter's friendship assiduously in an effort, he told himself, to bring the village eventually back under one roof and into one temple. Thus, while such a regathering of the fold had yet to occur in spite of Marcus Hawkins's continued admonitions that it would one day happen, the good minister was universally well spoken of and invited, often with his wife, to every house in the village at least once a year. As he stepped into Peter's cottage, he was a man equally as much out to see an old friend as to comfort a bereaved family.

"Peter, Peter," said Marcus Hawkins, shedding his coat as he entered out of the rain and stood carefully in the hallway while Rachel took his coat and hung it on the wall rack.

"Peter, I am so glad to see you, and Rachel too, always so lovely and full of health." He removed his rubbers and, after embracing Rachel, shook Peter's hand with both of his own and moved assuredly toward the sitting room, with Peter slightly ahead of him, into the warmer glow of the oil lamp.

"I'll go," Rachel said, "and fetch Beth for dinner. Peter, you and Marcus talk some and we'll be along right soon." She disappeared into the gloom of the stairs.

"Perhaps I should go with her," the minister responded, starting to rise from the large, overstuffed chair in which he had already seated himself.

"No, no, don't bother just yet, Marcus. It'll hold. The boy's in a high fever and a bit out of his head. You could do no good up there." Peter handed Hawkins a glass of wine and sat down himself. He watched the neatly manicured fingers of the clergyman close around the glass and felt vaguely embarrassed by his own rough, reddened hands.

"I'll go up later then, Peter, and see if I can help some before I go. The Lord works strangely, Peter. I'll do what I can."

Here Marcus Hawkins stopped and sipped his wine. Then, after a pause, he sighed and began again.

"There's a ship out there, Peter." He turned and looked out the window, over the now almost obscured dunes. "Heard of it as I got ready to come over here. Gabriel came to tell me before he left for the station. There'll be plenty of work out there tonight, and you and I had best pray for those poor lost souls so in need of the Lord's help this day."

⚓ ⚓ ⚓

Ezekiel stood along the beach where Gabriel Midgett and his crew were working desperately against the storm. He could hear Deborah's moan, low and frantic within his ear. He had watched the ship run hard aground off the shoal, a ship, he felt, much like the one that must have made that terrible passage to the new lands so long ago, carrying his grandma and so many others. Even the storm seemed right. Outraged it was at all that had happened so long ago. Lord Jesus knew. Suffering in this world did not go unrewarded in Heaven, that was sure. Just like those people out there wailing and calling for help (he could see them even as he could hear them). It might not come in this world, but for certain in the next.

*Calamar*, that was her name. He could barely make it out in the approaching darkness, the gray, angry sea obscuring his vision. She stood two or three hundred feet offshore within an angry ocean. She had come ashore ponderously and beached almost immediately upon the shoals. The sea was already filled with floating wreckage from the great barkentine as it lay whipped and scourged by the sea around it. Already its sails and masts were gone, down to the courses, and huge waves were tossing pieces of lumber ashore, end over end upon the surfmen.

✦ ✦ ✦

Marcus was speaking with sententious levity. "Looks like that palmetto of yours is going to get torn apart again, Peter." Marcus wanted to lighten the evening some, but Peter Wahab was not speaking much. No wonder, though, no wonder. "Course it does come back every year now, isn't that so?"

"Yes," said Peter. "Somehow the winter never gets to the core of her. I've never bothered to trim the dead fronds all these years. Always thought maybe that helps some."

"Maybe so, maybe so, but it always has seemed a miracle to me how that old tree makes it every year. Shouldn't be here, just shouldn't. Well, you know that, don't you?"

Where were those women? Marcus thought. Where were

they? These times were always so hard. He always felt so awkward.

❧ ❧ ❧

Somewhere he had seen all this before, Ezekiel felt, seen it all, the terrible wind, full gale strength, an inferno, sails torn and flapping wildly, crew and passengers helpless before the storm's rage.

"We're lost, my God, we're lost. Oh, God, God, help us!"

On the beach, the woman's terror-filled voice could not be heard, but Ezekiel knew it was there.

Ezekiel heard the screeching of timber as the ship's supports twisted and wrenched against the storm.

"Lord, what a night for dyin'," he heard Mr. Gabriel yell. "When's that damn Lyle gun gonna get up here?"

❧ ❧ ❧

"Ah!"

The women were coming down at last, thank the Lord. Marcus Hawkins rendered silent gratitude for his deliverance from this morose man across from him. Rachel, plain though she was, had never left him to carry on a conversation alone, and all he'd been able to get from Peter was a few words about the palmetto. Beth, of course, was forever a joy, pretty and alert, never one to burden others with her troubles. Ah well, some people's greatness was cast upon them unsought. If Peter needed his help, it would be forthcoming. Marcus rose from his chair.

"Well, I'm sorry we took so long." Rachel looked worried. "I do hope you enjoyed the wine, Reverend. Shall we go in to dinner? Beth and I will bring in the fixin's."

"Rachel, I declare, there's no such rush." Above all, Marcus wanted to be gracious, to be kind. "We're in no hurry for those good fixin's of yours. Well, I mean we certainly do look forward to them, but not as much as to your company. Don't bother yourself so and sit down with us a moment. Peter, pour your wife and Beth a glass of wine."

"Well, I-I . . . ." Rachel stuttered.

"You stay for a minute, Rachel," Beth broke in. "I'll tend to the kitchen."

"No, Beth, no . . . ."

"I'd love to stay, Reverend, but Isaac is poorly upstairs, and I don't want to leave him too long. Please go on without me."

"Oh, I see. Why—yes, of course. I should have realized." This was bad. Certainly he should have seen the situation more clearly. Hawkins swayed graciously above the still-seated Peter. "Let's all of us take our wine to the table, then, and I'll visit Isaac after supper. These are doubtless trying days on us all. It's been a bad winter."

Silently, the four of them went in to supper. Peter carried the wine tray to the sideboard, filled and placed four goblets, and then seated himself at the head of the table with Minister Hawkins on his right and Beth on his left. Job, he remembered, had exported yaupon tea from the Banks. Rachel brought in the meal and then sat down herself.

"I've never seen the likes of your cooking, Rachel, never. Never, that is, except when Beth Turner is at her very best, and then she does give you a run." Marcus Hawkins looked over the table at both women and smiled amiably. He was more at home now and did want to please these fine, simple women who worked so hard and endured their lives with such courage and strength. The dinner was a very special one for him. Rachel had even opened some brandied peaches that she must have been saving just for such a time. He was humbled and grateful.

"Peter, would you like to lead the responsive reading tomorrow?"

Peter assented with a nod and the minister continued.

"Good, good. It's much better on lay Sunday if I get in the way as little as possible, don't you think? After all," said Hawkins proudly, "preaching is not one of my strong points as a minister, especially when we've a man with your voice and learning. I'll perform the call to worship, introduce you at the end of my announcements, and give the benediction. Other than that, it's all up to you."

Again, Peter absently nodded his assent. He wondered what hymns might be sung. "Rock of Ages" maybe, or "Blessed Assurance." He liked those. Liked them a great deal.

"Rachel, what a fine dinner. I can't say it enough. Why, even when I was in Raleigh years ago, they didn't have cooking like this." Marcus discreetly sipped his wine.

"Surely those Raleigh folk can outdo us Bankers in somethin', can't they?" said Beth, smiling. The superiority of the islands was Marcus Hawkins's favorite subject with his congregation.

"Why, surely so, Beth. They can outpolitic us any day, and they've all those government agencies up there."

Rachel actually laughed. "Let's hope we never get good at such things, Reverend." It was common island bias, held in good humor.

"Yes, that's true, Rachel—but a table like this, and in such company—I'm always reminded of those years. There's something so wholly civilized about it. Something you can't get any other way."

*   *   *

The ship would soon be fully split in two. Ezekiel watched with tense excitement.

Far away, over the roar of the surf, someone called again for a Lyle gun in order to shoot a line out to the ship. "Can't row out in that surf," he said. "It'll kill us all."

But until the gun arrived, they would have to try, and the gun would not be there for some time. Couldn't move the gun quickly in this storm, not over the beaches now. By morning, there wouldn't be much beach left, thought Ezekiel. A storm like this took its toll every time.

> *The Lord hath purposed to destroy*
> *the wall of the daughter of Zion;*
> *He hath stretched out a line;*
> *He hath not withdrawn*
> *His hand from destroying.*

Again he strained to hear the staccato cries that came from the ship, over the wrathful sea. How hard that voyage had been, Deborah had said long ago, how many had died.

> *Arise, cry out in the night:*
> *in the beginning of the watches*
> *pour out thine heart like water*
> *before the face of the Lord.*

And Deborah was there dying, clutching unseen within her hand the heritage of centuries. But everyone knew what was in it. Her face beautiful even in the last agony.

> *Look not upon me, because I am black,*
> *because the sun hath looked upon me.*
> *I am black but comely, as the tents of Kedar.*

The night closed utterly upon him, and Ezekiel could discern only the fitful movement of lamps and the cries of castaways.

✦ ✦ ✦

"I remember, too, when I was in England with my mother," said the Reverend over dessert. "There, indeed, is a civilized country, one John Wesley could proudly call home. The smell of perfume and green grass at Kensington . . . ."

"Those places are so far away," mused Rachel.

"Why, Marcus Hawkins, a body'll get to think you're not content on Ocracoke," teased Beth.

"No, no, not at all. We're very lucky upon these islands, mark my word. You all know how I've grown to love it here so, but the Lord puts many temptations in our way." The Reverend fingered his gold cuff link. He pressed the silver fork deeply into the cake before him.

"Job once told me he bought that silver for Judith. It was to be a wedding present for her."

Everyone turned toward the head of the table.

"Why, you never told me that," Rachel said. Her voice quavered slightly.

"I just now remembered," Peter said. He continued to stare blankly at Marcus Hawkins's fork. The minister laid it upon his plate. "Job was like that. I don't guess he ever told Judith."

"My Lord, how strange," said Beth.

"Why would he keep such a thing from his own daughter?" Rev. Hawkins's fingers played with his lips. The situation was becoming too tactile, too intimate. He felt like a Peeping Tom about to discover nakedness through a window. But one must talk. Sound itself was protective.

"I don't know . . . I really don't. Once when I was sick, he whispered about it to me, about riches stored up for us, about what was waiting for me. He said Judith had given up her silver and gold, that the elders were right."

"An apocryphal story, no doubt." Marcus grinned as he looked around the table. No one laughed. He hadn't really expected them to laugh, he decided. But anything to get Peter away from this. It was so unlike him. Peter should have laughed. Peter should have appreciated the wit.

But Peter was lost in the maze of his own memories. Old

Wahab had given forty per cent of his earnings, a full tithe for every family member, to the church. Job had moved the warehouses to Portsmouth after Racer's Storm in '37, gathering riches. And old Howard had bought land for ten dollars an acre in '74, donating part of it for the new school, along with Pharaoh.

"Silver and gold, a rich heritage," Peter said. "Rachel, they were your wedding presents. That's what he meant."

"Oh, Peter, no, no! Job had so much more than just money. Why, there isn't a family around doesn't remember some debt to Job Wahab. Why, what about the time he got that flamingo from Florida brought up just for little Joanne Williams, that year she was so sickly?"

"Treasure of the Nile, he called it." Peter was staring abstractedly past the lit candles. "It never lived the year out."

The conversation had nowhere to go. It was a dead end, a cul-de-sac of painful and dangerous memories, thought Marcus. He must get up and see the boy and then go home to Rebecca. As it was, the storm was blowing hard, and he probably shouldn't have come out on a night like this at all. People are so fragile, he thought to himself, they need so much tending and care. Ah, Lord help us all.

"Well," Marcus began, "I've been told that Pharaoh Wahab was an upright and God-fearing man. The waste of a flamingo now and then is hardly a mortal fault. I'm sure Job intended it to live, and he was trying to do good. Flamingoes," the Reverend mused happily. "How can one blame him? Flamingoes and peacocks. Why, they were all over England when I was there, the zoos and what. Most civilized, most ancient of birds, I think. I—"

"No! No!"

Marcus strained in the dim light and saw Peter Wahab's red and enraged face leaning at him out of the darkness at the edges of the table, livid behind the candlelight.

"No, it won't be! Do you hear, it won't be. What's Kensington or London to me? Where are they anyway? Can I touch them and feel them? What's Raleigh to me and all your civilization and fine manners? What do I care for them—or Job or Judith? Job told me how he loved her and wished to forgive her."

"Peter, Peter, forgive what, dear?" He was hurting, Rachel saw. She could do so little for the looming shadow across the table. "Forgive what?" she asked again, rising from her chair but not moving toward him.

"I don't know, I don't know. And does it matter? She left us. We're not the elders. There is no sin to be punished. Not in this house. You all think that Isaac will die. How can you do that? How can you? He is my son—do you hear?—the flesh of my flesh, the blood of my blood, the holy and secret part of my soul. God— God— What can you do? I can't give him toys to play with, peacocks and flamingoes."

A draft chilled the room, and the candles flickered. Marcus Hawkins looked down at his cuff link and played nervously with his napkin ring.

"But, no! No!" Peter fairly screeched. "This will not be! My God will not allow this! I have faith in his goodness and He will not desert me! Do you hear? He will not desert me, his good and loyal servant."

No one answered him.

"Yes—ah—yes, Peter," said Marcus finally, in order to break the silence. Friendship could go no further. "Like you, we have never doubted that. God's will be done, and I pray for you every night. Now let me see young Isaac for just a minute before I must leave and get home to Rebecca. She'll be missing me and it is a nasty night."

There was nothing more to be said. Indeed, Marcus feared that he had already said too much and that Peter might lose control again in his wildness and frenzy. Death was always so hard to bear. They all got up and left the table in silence. The minister went upstairs with Rachel to see the boy while Beth slowly and carefully cleared the dishes. Peter went into the sitting room and stared out the window into the storm-darkened night. No one spoke to him until Reverend Hawkins came down from the sickroom with Rachel. Beth went into the kitchen and returned to Isaac's room with a pan of hot water and towels. Hawkins took his leave, saying that he would see everyone at church tomorrow, and then turned into the storm.

That night, Peter slept poorly. He failed to finish his sermon and tossed and turned constantly in bed, attempting in his dreams to mold the few, final sentences. In spite of his promise and admonition, Rachel stayed with Beth most of the night. The two took turns tending the fevered boy, who now kept calling out for his parents and brothers, often gagging, his small chest heaving as he doubled in pain while wavelike chills regularly tore at his small, now frail body.

*** 

Outside, unknown to anyone, Ezekiel had found a refuge from the storm in Peter's stable. He lay on straw next to the warm body of an island pony and dreamed of great, gleaming, watery cities; of ivory thrones; of seven stars and golden candelabras; of Deborah in fine, white linen and the raiment of queens; and of a storm.

# VI

# REVERDIE

✶ ✶ ✶

AND ONCE there was the great hurricane that came down upon the islands (Ezekiel knew). It had arrived so unexpectedly in June of a year long ago that nobody had taken account of the high seas that began running from the southeast off the Cape on a fine, warm, sunny Wednesday morning just like this one. Ezekiel had noticed it though; all day he had sat by the shore below Hatteras Light, sometimes trying to paint but more often casting a worried look toward the sea and watching the huge waves that formed far out on the horizon and swept inexorably landward, mounting larger and larger until they eventually broke upon the shoals with an increasingly terrific roar. Ezekiel hadn't liked the way the sea was mounting up over the shoals, in spite of the calm, oppressive warmth of the day. He hadn't liked the slight shift in the direction of the waves as they ran shoreward and slapped hard against the sand. And most of all, he hadn't liked the color and smell of the water itself. It wasn't a clear, lucid green but a dirty and cloudy brown, full of shells, weeds, and drifting debris.

So Ezekiel had stopped his painting and started building an elaborate sand castle far inshore, south of the Cape. The tide had been running high all week, and he'd noticed that too; but now he decided to build a castle a full five feet beyond the highest tide he could remember, where the sand was so dry and without substance that he had to use his old bait pail to carry water up to the spot and wet the sand himself. All day long he worked on his castle. The men in the lighthouse at the Cape's point occasionally saw him from their superior height, but it was only "ole nigger Zeke with his ass in the sand again."

"Old Zeke likes dirty water," a young Buxton boy mused while looking out to sea. "Boy, must've been one hell of a kill out there."

Ezekiel never heard them. He kept building the castle and looking out to sea all through the afternoon and the long, languid summer evening. When the castle walls finally fell, pressed upon by their own enormous weight or dried out by the sun, he simply started again, spreading large Saharan plains around his castle and building tiny, fearsomely grotesque huts within the huge castle walls, with grass for trees within the courtyards and perfectly cylindrical bastions on all four corners of the moated walls. Past the stick drawbridge within the walls, his huts formed intricate cities around a large, elaborately decorated keep—but Ezekiel very rarely got this far before his civilization failed itself and he would have to begin anew with his long stretches of plain and palmettos penetrating into the deeper and thicker wilderness of the sea oats themselves, carrying unknown shadows of Songhay and the Niger.

For five days Ezckiel continued his vigil. He would leave only late at night, find a bite to eat at the back door of Howard's store, and sleep fitfully on his lone cot in old Abraham Midgett's workshop. Next morning, he would get up, drink a cup of coffee in the kitchen before the family rose, leave the coffee kettle warming over the fire, take a biscuit with him, pick up his odd assortment of hooks, lines, paints, picks, and the rest, and run to the Cape. His castle would be dry and in ruins beneath a warm, morning sun. Then he would kneel down and build again.

On the fifth morning, however, Ezekiel noticed that the wind, now blowing from the east, had changed direction drastically. His castle was there, in ruins as before, but this time it was wet, with solid clumps of wet sand where the castle's walls and turrets had once been. Except during a storm, the sea had never been this high in all of Ezekiel's life, and now he was positive that what God had asked him to suffer through these last days was about to be consummated. Here on this lonely and forsaken coast, God had chosen him, an old nigger, to warn the chosen of the flock. If destruction was to come, then the just must be told, and old Ezekiel was to be God's appointed messenger. To him had been given the vision. The tide had never in all history come this high before, and it could only be because a great storm, the tool of

God's divine justice, was waiting off the coast, waiting until the Lord made the vision complete—to Ezekiel, his loving servant. It would purge the evils from men's souls and show them the power of God—God himself. Ezekiel would wait no longer. He gazed quickly at his ruined and absurd castle, then turned and ran for the village.

It was not to the people of Hatteras that Ezekiel ran, however; it was to the children of Ocracoke. His vision told him so. As he ran over the hard, compacted sand, now washed white by the early morning sunlight, Ezekiel remembered the sins of the unjust, of those who had failed to live by God's law, and of King Pharaoh; and he remembered the Seven Sisters and how they had brought this retribution upon the islands. The sea was rough now, and the morning wind brought a tumult to the beach. In disarray, the gulls cried sharply overhead, and Ezekiel ran quickly, ducking his head in order to avoid their frenzied and erratic flight, once falling in the sand and tasting its warm, salty putrescence. The world became quick to Ezekiel. He knew the gulls and the lonely sandpipers were agents of the Almighty. They touched his skin with spirit and flame.

He thought of his own malefaction, when as a little boy Ezekiel had been carrying hot water for Miz Ruth Ann Granger (Mr. Gabriel's distant cousin, she was). Miz Ruth was an inlander from Elizabeth City and had been staying the summer with Miz Mary and Mister Abraham. She was unmarried at thirty-one; unmarried, and folks talked. Miz Ruth had stopped him in the empty house and told him to fill a hot bath. Then, after Ezekiel had finished with the last kettleful, she'd stopped him and told him to get some towels upstairs.

It was early evening. Abraham and the family had just left for a town meeting. Ezekiel found the towels and brought them downstairs into the kitchen. Miz Ruth, almost naked, was seated on a chair, the dark, nigger color of her pubic hair clearly visible beneath a long, whalebone corset. Ezekiel stopped at the doorjamb and stared. He knew what a cunt was; at nine he was old enough to have even touched and fondled Jessie Clair one night in the deep, wet grass behind Wilson's barn. But Jessie was a nigger like him, and the twelve-year-old Jessie had not had such a luxuriance of hair as Miz Ruth. He continued to stare, so frightened he could neither enter nor leave the room. Then Miz Ruth, smiling as if patronizingly amused by his worship, called him to her.

"Come here, Ezekiel," she said. "You must help me with my bath. Come, come, my corset needs unlacing. Be a good boy and do as I say."

Ezekiel had moved slowly and awfully in silent trespass. He helped unlace the thick, stiff corset, set it down on a chair in the corner, and got the soap from the sink as she stepped into the tub. Then she made him come over to her and help wash her, laughing softly at his unspoken fear. She guided his trembling hands over her shoulders and neck. "Get some more water and soap on the cloth, Ezekiel. How can you get me clean without water and soap?" Then she laughed again and called him "Saucer-eyes." "Haven't you ever seen a girl, Ezekiel? Oh, I bet you've played with some little pickaninnies, now haven't you? Tell me about them, Ezekiel. Were they like me? Were they soft and white like me, Ezekiel? Did they have these big, soft things I have, child? Tell me, Ezekiel. Don't be afraid."

And all this time she continued to guide his hands down along her arms and over her large, rounded breasts, which moved ponderously under his touch as his hand glided over the stiff, erect nipples. He said nothing, though, not even when she put his hand down between her legs and he felt the strange, wiry softness of her hair. He said nothing, and she, softly moaning, tightened her legs around his hand and told him to wash her well, pushed his hand along her thighs and stomach, and looked toward the ceiling, her eyes closing every so often, her body shuddering beneath his hand. Ezekiel was sweating with terror and rage when she finally let him go—all the while laughing and smiling at him.

Yes, that surely was transgression, sin, everlasting shame upon his own black soul. From the moment he walked through the door, he knew (and so did she) that he would never speak of it, never confess this profane love.

Thus, as he ran through Hatteras toward the island's southern tip, Ezekiel didn't warn the people about the storm. Instead, he took Matthew Wilson's old, leaky skiff, which had not been used for months and was stowed outside of town on the western side of the point, still smelling of fish; and he rowed across the small inlet which then separated the two islands. To atone for his sin, Ezekiel would save the people of God's town, not those of Hatteras, who had lived in abomination.

When he finally reached Ocracoke island, Ezekiel's arms and back ached terribly. He could easily have run across the inlet in five or ten minutes; but it had taken him fully four hours in the dinghy, and he couldn't remember how many times he had almost capsized in the rough, mounting seas. Ezekiel thanked God fervently for his deliverance as he ran down the center of the island, avoiding the beach. Every quarter mile he stopped, his mouth twisted and open, gasping for air that seemed never enough. Sometimes he would trip and fall, only to pick himself up and continue. He knew he must reach town. He ran until his forehead felt cold and his fingers tingled. As his running became awkward and lethargic, Ezekiel prayed the very oak and cedar to help him on his way. God's things would help. He must reach town soon (Ezekiel knew). It was getting on toward afternoon, and there was much to be done. Perhaps the Lord was even now preparing his children, knowing as He did Ezekiel's weakness.

When he arrived in town it was early evening, and the sea

was running full high with great whitecaps on the waves and a strong, easterly wind. It had taken Ezekiel nine hours to cover the twenty-six miles between Cape Hatteras and Ocracoke town, and he was afraid that he was too late. Surely everyone must be preparing for it.

But they weren't. As Ezekiel burst into Bob Howard's store, he was shocked to find so many men and women still leisurely buying groceries or linen goods, or merely chewing the fat. He couldn't understand. No one was worried? When he tried to tell young Bob about the storm, Bob just laughed and asked Ezekiel why he was "way down here where free meals are so hard to come by." Luke Taylor even carried on about the "good fishin' weather" coming up, and he lectured Bob on how to treat darkies.

"You might hurt his feelin's, Bob," Luke said. "After all, darkies is people too, and we out here on the island don't have so many of 'em that we can't afford a little kindness. Don't you worry, Zeke. If a storm hits we'll take care of you." And then he said in a sly voice so's the ladies across the room couldn't hear, "and that little fat-assed nigger gal you been sniffin' 'round up near the Wilsons', too."

Ezekiel stopped and stared dumbly at Luke Taylor. No one believed him; chosen of the Lord, but they would not believe. He looked around the store and saw everyone staring. Luke's daughter Samantha smiled solicitously while her father continued another dirty joke to the men at the counter. Ezekiel stumbled outside and down the main road, past the cove and the wharf. He tried to tell people of the coming storm, but old Ed Manners and Mark Terrell just laughed and asked since when did hurricanes visit the islands in June. "Nope, you're wrong this time," said Terrell. "A nigger can't be right every time, ya know. I look to see it get pretty heavy out there, Zeke, but no hurricane. None a-tall."

No one would listen. All over town Ezekiel was ignored.

Even old Job Wahab merely pursed his grizzled face and looked at the sky. But he did nothing. He did not praise the Lord as Ezekiel had thought he would. He did not offer up thanks. He just turned around and went inside his cottage, calling after him that Ezekiel could stay in the kitchen till the morrow if he wished.

The storm came late that night. It was brutal and vicious beyond endurance and beyond hope. At nine o'clock the wind was still a strong, steady breeze from the east, but by ten it was blowing a gale, and by eleven it was so terrible and fearsome that even Ezekiel, miserable and confused, was forced to seek shelter underneath an old, long-unused whaleboat tied down and stored in Luke Taylor's barn. All night long under the boat and through the next day, Ezekiel prayed and moaned for the people of Ocracoke. He had tried to warn them; but they had not listened, and the storm thus wreaked a frightening vengeance. People were caught trying to board doors and windows in the middle of the night. Boats had been left unsecured, and livestock were still grazing on the island's open, sparse grasslands. Whole houses were struck down, and boats were splintered against the wharves as though some huge child's hand had perversely strewn them around the cove.

Two great ships went down off the Diamond Shoals that night, Ezekiel remembered. Another went down off Lookout, and one just below Cape Fear. In all, 133 people died on those ships; none were saved. It was the greatest hurricane ever to come up the coast, and long after, people often talked of winds as high as 175 miles an hour at the storm's worst. Before the storm crossed the Banks, its circular winds almost emptied Pamlico Sound of water, and after it crossed them, there was sea flooding as far inland as Williamston and Greenville. Tides were twenty feet above normal, and Hatteras Inlet widened half a mile before midday Monday.

The eye had crossed directly over Hatteras, and the town was almost leveled before the storm left. Daniel Howard's new store was carried intact more than a mile into the Sound and then left sitting there in ten feet of water on a sandbar that had not existed the day before. The Methodist Church, the one stone building in town, lost all its windows, its roof, and had three huge fissures in its south and east walls, the east wall actually peeling away from the south corner, toppling askew as though the creation of a maniac architect, without reason, without rhyme (but Ezekiel knew). Such was God's justice.

# VII

# THE
# AWFUL PROMISE

PETER AWOKE in the morning to find the storm much abated. He dressed carefully, seeing to it that his collar was straight and unwrinkled and his spotless white cuffs perceptible below the clean black of his suit coat. Only on Sundays was he so meticulous with his clothes and dress, although

Rachel had often told him that he was too fussy and picky.

"Your trousers are in the wash more than they are on your legs, Peter Wahab," she would say, a brightness in her eyes as if he had not married a proper and neat girl who always looked her best.

The curtains swayed as he opened the bedroom door, and Peter felt a chill. He passed quickly by Isaac's room and walked noiselessly down the stairs. In the kitchen, breakfast was prepared for him, hot coffee close by the fire, grits, bacon and eggs. Rachel was not there.

He ate quickly since they would need him early at church and spilled some coffee on the table, scalding his wrist. He put butter on the burn and then looked everywhere for a towel with which to dry the table and floor, only to find it neatly folded over the back of his chair. He sat down and grimly finished breakfast. The incomplete sermon worried him, but he found it impossible to concentrate. Had the ship aground off the island weathered the night? How strange it must be to face the fury of the sea with safety in sight but not in hand and a fine harbor just yards away on the leeward side of the island. "Lord have mercy," he said as he rose, pushing the heavy oak chair back away from the table. Overhead, the floor creaked to the rhythmic motion of Rachel crossing from Isaac's bed to the fireplace.

"Or Beth," he said to himself as he hurried quietly through the hallway and out the door. "Or Beth. It could have been Beth."

Outside, the wind was down considerably, and the rain struck only in short, unexpected bursts against his thin raincoat. Overhead, the whitening clouds hurried southward, gigantic misshapen creatures, which seemed to wind themselves into an intricate, inhuman allegory that he found himself unable either to understand or to touch. They tortured themselves into such misbegotten shapes, so arbitrary, so evanescent, as unalterable as life itself, yet so changing and

*The Awful Promise* / 95

temporary, so lacking in substance as not to exist at all. It caused Peter acute pain to realize that minutes from—moments from—then, the huge, ungainly serpent that arched its long, shifting bulk high above its more abject neighbors would be gone. The cloud collapsed and fell quickly earthward, for there were few cathedral vaults in this sky.

Peter walked toward the muddied, opened gate. Sand. Sand was everywhere. The islands were built upon it, as shifting as the clouds, as capricious as the sea itself. Each storm proved the fearful temporariness of the islands, their especially contrived nature. Even the resurrection fern, which he now stared at, was not native to the islands. But it, too, had mutated in order to endure the killing cold of winter.

"It certainly blew a gale of wind last night," Peter said softly to himself as he closed the gate and latched it. He wanted to walk out upon the island to the beach and see the changes the storm must surely have wrought. Entire hills were often moved by storms the likes of this one. The beach was most explicitly the handiwork of the wind and the sea. If there was an allegory in the clouds, then what did the beach tell a man? Peter mused as he walked down the path, his mind grasping an image only to forget it moments later and wandering increasingly amid vague abstractions.

The morning had gone badly. In truth, the night had gone badly too. Isaac had gotten worse, his cough a kind of intense shudder, more of a choking than a cough. He had cried out for Peter between the violent spasms that tore at his chest.

Hadn't Beth said it was pneumonia? How could it be pneumonia if Isaac had diphtheria? Had Beth explained that? Or how could his son's heart be affected? Isaac had always been a strong boy. That was good, Beth said. It would certainly help him when the crisis came.

All the while, Peter had refused to enter the sickroom, even when he clearly heard Isaac calling him over the wind's more constant shrieking.

*"Whence art thou come?"* said
   the holy man.
*"From a putrid drop,"* replied
   the student.
*"Whither thou art going?"*
*"To a place of dust, worm and maggot."*
*"And before whom are thou destined
   to give an accounting?"*
*"Before the King of kings of kings,
   the Holy One, blessed be He."*

The sand slipped beneath his feet, loose and watery. It made him awkward and slow. He hoped Rachel would understand. She had been so frantic, so uncompromising during the night.

"For God's sake, Peter," she had screamed, "for God's sake, he's your own son, your own first-born and last son. Are you not to comfort him in this hour? Where is your love?"

She had leaned heavily against the bannister for support, her throat making inarticulate, gasping sounds, the railing squeaking as it bent under her weight. Suddenly afraid she would fall, he grabbed her shoulders and held her firmly. How he hated her. Passionately, his own breath heavy, his body aching. Why would she not leave him alone? Why was she forcing this dreadful intimacy upon him? Her so obvious weakness disgusted him as if the tallow of a candle had gone bad, pervading the house with some strange and noxious odor. He could not, he would not, go into that room. Isaac would live! Only to show weakness now, to fail in his faith, would make it untrue.

His hands squeezed Rachel's shoulders until she cried out sharply against the pain. Relaxing, holding her at arm's length in the darkened hallway lit only by the open doorway at their backs, they stared at one another as if surprised by their own flesh. The sallow whiteness of Rachel's breast was visible between the wide lapels of her housecoat. Dirt and tears streaked her face. The empty doorway glowed luridly within the night.

"No, Rachel," he heard himself whisper. "No, I will not go in! Have you so little faith?"

Tired and abject, she pulled free of his grasp and put her hands against the wall. "God. Oh, God. What am I to do? God, dear God! God, what must I do?"

She pushed the thin strands of her hair back from her face and turned back towards Isaac's room. Beth was at the doorway now, her long, slender arms beckoning to Rachel.

"He will live, Beth," Peter called. "Make her understand."

But now Peter was cold; the wind tore at his coat and chilled him to the bone. He felt lonely and tired. The village was empty, it seemed, and as he turned at the end of the road, the wind off the harbor whipped about him and seared his face. Never had the village looked so dreary. The few dinghies along the water's edge tossed wildly as each capricious burst of weather fell over them. Peter shivered. How completely this place was his own. There was no one else. Even the few people whom he now saw, far off, entering church in ones and twos seemed pitiful and helpless. Yet, he thought, insular and desolate, the village waited century after century, sequestered by the ocean's irresolvable shore.

And he, himself, walked apart within, never really at one with, the harsh, white walls of the church to which he had devoted so much of his life. Obdurate! Strange that it should stand so stubborn and unrelenting upon this island. Only the supple trees could dance in the wind, he thought. One must yield to it. There could be no presumption.

That was it! One must yield to God's love. Peter greeted Jessie Terrell and her three children who, bedraggled and wet from their long walk, skipped unconcernedly up the steps of the church.

"Slow down a bit, you young'uns," Jessie called good-naturedly at them as she lifted her skirt and walked up the steps beside Peter. "The Lord will wait for us all."

Yes, yes, thought Peter vaguely. Perhaps that was the ending to his sermon. One could not be haughty here. God's love would not have it. The contumelious would certainly be struck down.

Peter prepared for the service quickly and efficiently, as he had done so many times before. The pews were only half-full and the church chilly. The wetness of the storm had seeped into the very clothes he now wore. He shivered.

How cold little Thomas had been that day so long ago (and Christmas only a short time away). Thomas, who loved to chase the fiddlers into their holes. How he would squat before their holes and cry, and he would not be comforted.

> *And if he shall neglect to hear them,*
> *tell it unto the church:*
> *but if he neglect to hear the church* . . . .

Little Thomas playing there, Rachel's favorite. They all knew that, even she did, petting him so and taking him upon her lap.

✯ ✯ ✯

Rachel was weeping now. How awful it all sounded. Elizabeth placed a cold compress upon his forehead. He was suffering, his body turning and twisting as if on a rack. And he didn't know her. She was sure of it. That terrible wheezing, the drawing in of breath as if he couldn't get any air.

✯ ✯ ✯

> *Verily I say unto you, that ye*
> *which have followed me* . . .
> *ye also shall sit upon twelve*
> *thrones* . . . *shall receive a*

*hundredfold, and shall inherit everlasting life.*

"Yes, Lord," Peter whispered to himself, as he walked in cadence down the aisle, Minister Hawkins by his side, the rhythms demanding his answers, "help me to love with compassion, and bereft of fear, leave me—my soul upon this barren waste to do thy bidding."

The hymn moved on, its tones strong and urgent. "This is my Father's world, and to my listening ears all nature sings while round me rings . . . ."

"But do not leave me alone, O Lord. Do not visit me so." Outside the windows, huge clouds massed, convulsed, and were swept beyond the sill. Inside, the line slowed as it reached the altar rail and the choir members moved toward their seats. Rachel would be sewing now, minding the boy. With Elizabeth at home, there would be no trouble. He had not seen the boy before he left, but all would be calm. The storm was abating. Rain chattered against the windows as a gust of wind blew over the church. The building shuddered as if alive.

Two days ago. It was two days ago that he had last touched Isaac. God, so long ago. The skin had shivered underneath his hand, and he had quickly withdrawn his fingers and pulled the blankets closer around the boy's neck. He had seemed so quiet, so profoundly tired and asleep.

"This is my Father's world, I rest me in the thought . . . ."

The church was still not as full as usual. Gabriel and many of the men remained out on the beach. Why? Why weren't they present? The choir stopped, and Marcus began the invocation in his long, nasal tones, carefully metered pauses accentuating its rote familiarity. "The Lord is in His holy temple . . . ."

Measure, measure and length and repetition, the habit of years. Order and pattern. Generations to remember by.

Invocation! Adoration! Affirmation! These were measures, measures of love— Yes! Lord, now it came to him, that which had so constantly eluded him last night. Invocation! Adoration! Affirmation! And then thanksgiving! A holy triune which brought grace and mercy. Inevitably brought these things as well! That was important. Thus only thanksgiving, only *it* was a proper form of worship. He rose for the responsive readings, staring in triumph toward the white walls of the church.

"He that dwelleth in the secret place of the Most High, shall abide under the shadow of the Almighty."

"I will say unto the Lord, He is my refuge and my fortress: my God; in Him will I trust."

Only in adoration did one lose pride completely. Peter wanted to kneel, to hold tightly the wooden bench and pray to Almighty God, his Father, the rock of his salvation. He wanted to press his knees hard into the hardness of the floor, to bless God, to rejoice in such complete and absolute submission, to rejoice in the gladness of days that must surely follow.

"Because he hath set his love upon me, therefore will I deliver him: I will set him on high because he hath known my name."

✦ ✦ ✦

Ezekiel looked back, grimaced, and lifted a dirty sleeve to shield his face. He hesitated to enter the front door of Peter's house. He was accustomed to the back, but it was locked against the wind. The front door would be open, though; he had seen Peter leave by it. Now he must go in. Over the fits of storm he heard Rachel crying. Elizabeth Turner was there, too, Ezekiel heard as he opened the door—she who had nursed him some years back at old man Midgett's when he'd caught that terrible winter cold. It had felt strange to have a white

## The Awful Promise / 101

woman treating him so. Long after, he had painted a gleam of white within a midnight blue sky and found a black tide flowing beneath them.

✦ ✦ ✦

"He shall call upon me and I will answer him: I will be with him in trouble; I will deliver him, and honor him."

Peter answered. "With long life will I satisfy him and show him my salvation."

Marcus next rose and made the announcements. Surely Gabriel was on the beach with all the other men of the lifesaving station. There was cause to rejoice. As of yet, no one had drowned during the night. The ship had not broken up completely, and a line had been successfully fastened to it some few hours ago. The transfer of crew and passengers was surely taking place this very minute. After church, all should prepare to house the survivors and show Christian kindness to them, for by some miracle it seemed that all would be saved.

Such things could happen. Peter looked out over the congregation as Marcus completed the few other weekly announcements. Such things did happen.

Little Sandy Williams shifted testily in her seat, pulling her stockings up (her dress with them) and brushing her hair smooth. Sunlight broke briefly through a window onto the center aisle and then faded away. The ushers moved in businesslike fashion from pew to pew. The choir began to sing.

Peter repeated the words to himself, "Love divine all love compelling, love my heart . . . ."

What was it last week? A beam from heaven that light. A beam, a beam, from, from— No, to, a beam of, of— Yes, "A beam of heaven, a vital ray, 'tis thine alone to give." Peter remembered. "How helpless guilty nature lies, unconscious of its load! The will perverse, the passions blind, in paths of ruin stray."

The ushers started forward from the back of the church.

"Can ought beneath a power divine the stubborn will subdue? To chase the shades of death away, and bid the sinner live." Peter was ready now to give his sermon. He waited through the doxology, then moved toward the pulpit.

⸙ ⸙ ⸙

Across town, Ezekiel was running. He was running to fetch Peter Wahab, whose son was sick unto death. Rachel had sent him, and a holy mission he knew it to be. "Ezekiel, Ezekiel, is that you?" she had said. Then, looking down on him from the head of the stairs, from darkness into darkness, the door closed behind him at the bottom of the stairs, she cried, "Oh, Lord, Ezekiel, go fetch Peter. Bring him here. His child is dying." She stopped, pressed her arms around her, and began to weep. Elizabeth Turner came out to hold her up.

"Stop, Rachel, stop," she said, but the crying continued.

"Oh, God—where is he, Beth? Where is he? Where are my children, Beth, my children?"

⸙ ⸙ ⸙

"Jesus asked," he intoned, " 'Do you love me?' And three times Peter responded, 'Yes, Lord.'

"As I sat here listening to the beautiful hymn we have just heard, I could not help remembering those days in Galilee. Three times the Lord asked of love and three times Peter told him 'Yes, Lord, I love you.' "

It seemed very right now, all these things he was saying. People in the pews stared at him. Not even Marcus could keep their attention as he could. This was God's gift, to speak the truth. Peter Wahab was sure of his power.

"Jesus wanted that love. He did not need it; his death was to be a perfect sacrifice, but He wanted love. For Peter's good, for man's life. 'Love divine all love compelling.'

"The apostle was not to be capable of so great a sacrifice, not to be found ready to die beside his Lord and Saviour." The church shuddered as another gust of wind struck it. "Yet in a short time, God's love was to appear utterly.

" 'To everything there is a season and a time to every purpose' saith the old, wise man, and this was Jesus' time, not Peter's. Peter was to deny his Lord, deny him thrice before the multitude and before God the Father, not capable of God's more consummate love. 'Be not rash with thy mouth,' it is said, 'and let not thine heart be hasty to utter anything before God.' Yet the fisherman whom Jesus loved so much was to do just this, to deny his Lord, to commit the most unworthy of sins, to be all but a Judas, his courage, his honesty failing him so completely at that last great moment. We can imagine Peter then, no better than the dust from which he rose, faced with the shameful presence of his own mortality before these last agonies of divine love, so consuming, so irrevocable in their finality. Remember that this was before the surety of resurrection, and even Peter stood ignorant before Jesus, ashamed and afraid."

There was a movement across one of the windows, darkness within the fitful sunlight.

"Yes, ignorant, ignorant of that very mortality, that human weakness, that very fear and sin that was man's invocation to God throughout the ages. We need Him, brethren. We need his love, his suffering, his knowledge, and his greater courage. God made man imperfect and weak, and we cannot live without his help and understanding. Divine love was not given to Peter. It is not given to man. We must call upon the Lord, humble ourselves, and invoke his name. Only then will He answer us; but answer us He must, for the song is true, the note everlasting: 'Love divine all love compelling.' God cannot refuse us. His love compels Him to save us from everlasting damnation if we truly and utterly trust in Him. God must suffer, suffer and die for our salvation."

Marcus shifted uneasily in his seat.

"So, brethren, we come to the second act in this trinity of love—adoration. For as surely as we must humble ourselves, as surely as divine love is not given to man and we must invoke God's help, which inevitably flows from perfect and divine love; so surely must man adore God, must worship Him in adoration, abject and supremely reverent before God Almighty's throne, prostrate in humility and joy. Our lives must be a daily litany to his mercy and grace. Jesus' death led not to the grave but to heaven, to salvation and resurrection. Peter could not have known that, but it was so. It was as certain as the Promised Land after forty years of wandering, as certain as the return from bondage, as certain as the Redeemer's own birth. It was inevitable!"

What was that? It was distracting, running from window to window, but Peter could not make out the figure. Peter's hands gripped the pulpit. He leaned toward the people, these people who were his now, his in this moment of passion and glory. He felt cold, rigid with anger and fury.

" 'We trust in the Lord, our God,' said Isaiah, and it is in that trust, that perfect surety, that we accomplish our trinity, for there we affirm our belief in divine justice" (that was wrong, wrong)—"divine mercy and love."

"Invocation, adoration, and affirmation. It is in this way that God's people come unto Him in completeness and oneness of spirit. Our presence here today attests God's love for us as surely as it proves our devotion to Him. Christ died to attest God's love for us—his forgiveness and grace. Upon that day of resurrection the power of evil and death was broken, the temple garment was rent, and the cross was proved triumphant. Peter's courage had failed, but not Christ's. Christ's love had been the conformity of heart, mind, and life to the will of God, the Father. That was his redemption of man, and our love must not be found wanting. We must accept...."

Bang! A gust of wind suddenly hit the church. The building shuddered. Marcus Hawkins looked up nervously from his polished shoes. A black figure was silhouetted, motionless within a western window. Peter stopped. For an instant, perceptible to no one but himself, he stared at the awful apparition. Outside, a tree cracked and splintered heavily to the ground. People turned in their seats and whispered uneasily to one another. It couldn't be. Peter knew it couldn't be.

"Love, then, love is our answer, our fortress and our only refuge." Peter felt his voice hollow and strangely protracted along the bare, white walls. "And to what does this love lead us? Where does the trinity take us? There can be only one answer. To thanksgiv...."

The church doors swung open and slammed wildly back and forth. Everyone, it seemed, in every pew of the church, turned to look. And Peter, frozen behind the pulpit, the very sign of his power and God's gift, felt himself powerless in a rage of terror. Up the center aisle of the church, his face red and raw from the weather but full of gladness and relief, strode Gabriel Midgett. His oilskins wet and dripping before the astonished congregation, Gabriel could not hide his joy.

"By God," he cried, "by the good Lord Almighty, we did it. The wind was peelin' the green out there all night and mornin', and we lost nary a one of 'em." An exclamation of relief, almost a cheer, filled the room. People talked quickly and excitedly to one another. Gabriel was awkward and childlike in his joy, his sense of victory and fulfillment. He searched almost in astonishment for his words. "God—we did it—those boys of our'n—they did it. No one like a Banker in a storm. It takes good men out there. You all can be proud . . . ."

"God bless us, God bless us all, Gabriel." Marcus Hawkins stood at the railing, looking benignly upon his parishioners, his face suffused with wonder and patriarchical approval.

Then Gabriel remembered his self-appointed mission. "We'll need beds, though, beds and houses, and hot food. Thirty-nine there was, thirty-nine in all, includin' three women and four young'uns. All safe, but cold and wet as eels. The boys are bringin' 'em in right now. They can't be but a mile or two up the beach. So let's make this a real joyous day for the Lord— God, all saved. You wouldn'ta believed the flaws blowin' in out there. Seventy, eighty mile an hour, I bet. Good Lord, we did it."

"Yes, good Lord above." The words rang through the church. Marcus started to raise his right hand, his cuff links polished and bright, to hold it out to these, his people in this hour of triumph.

"No! No! By God, no! It shall not, it will not be! By God in his damnable heaven, it will not be! No! No! No! No!"

Livid with rage, a rage that rendered dumb all those who saw and heard him, Peter Wahab was walking swiftly down the center aisle, heedless of Gabriel, of Marcus, of those assembled around him, toward the frantic yet timid figure who had entered the church unseen behind Gabriel Midgett and had remained silent and confused at the back of the church. In fearful ululation, Peter stared into the horrified and propitiatory eyes of Ezekiel.

"No! No! It cannot be so! As God is in his heaven, it must not be so! God damn you to bring me such news!" Peter cried over and over, clutching the old Negro by his jacket and hitting him again and again in a paroxysm of fear and despair.

Then Gabriel's strong, wet arms were holding Peter fast,

and Ezekiel was running out the door into the bright, crisp sunlight.

"Stop, Peter," Gabriel cried. "Oh Lord, I'm sorry, but it's not his fault. Leave off, man. Leave off."

Peter pulled himself free and turned to face his tormentor. But Gabriel was crying unashamedly. It was the only sound within the present, awful, looming silence of the place. Slowly, as if startled by some ineffable revelation, Peter backed to the door of the church, then turned, and walked swiftly away.

# VIII

# WEARER OF THE CROWN

PETER WALKED toward the cottage, a grim and remote mechanism. He felt that he was moving toward the end of all history, of life as he had known it for so long. As he took step after step, he looked to neither side. The storm was dying. His child was dead, the last of his four strong young sons, the last of this fourth generation of his name. He could not explain why, but he felt that it was so, with a blood certainty. Ezekiel's blurred face at the window had told him, when the poor old man, desperate to tell Peter of his son's dying, had hesitated to enter the church during the sermon and had stood outside the church, shy and trembling, absurdly fumbling with a streaked and soiled rain cap.

So Peter walked home, not to see the dead body of his son or even to comfort Rachel—she was distant and abstracted, hardly important to him now—but simply because there was nothing else to do. His pace slowed. There had been nothing else to do at the church except to beat upon the old Negro's body again and again until finally he was pulled away, Ezekiel still huddled upon his knees next to the doorjamb, crying and moaning. "Oh, Mister Peter, I know, I know. God knows I'm sorry for you. God knows, God knows." Peter had heard Ezekiel's chant and had looked about him. He had known he could not stay and endure the stares, the pity, the condescension of his neighbors, and so he had left. He had walked away because there was nothing else to do.

*Seven kinds of calamity come
upon the world for seven classes
of sin. Pestilence comes upon
the world for crimes punishable
by death . . . .*

Peter stood at the gateway to his house. And what crimes, he thought, were punishable by death? He could not remember. It was as if he had never known, so far away it all seemed. He fumbled with the red and rusted latch and pushed it up and down, up and down, a number of times. The palmetto tree was still standing, torn and ragged. He would pull it down this next year. There was no use for it any more.

Ezekiel remained outside the church as the people left it, going home now (he knew) to prepare for the survivors who would soon come from the beach. His arms and shoulders hurt from where Mr. Peter had hit him, and there was a small cut over his left eye. It stung whenever he looked up at the sky, but he didn't mind.

"Come round to the kitchen, Ezekiel," Gabriel Midgett said to him as he left the church, concluding his conversation with Marcus Hawkins and Lemuel Williams. Some of those saved would be put up at the hotel.

"After two or so," Gabriel called back. "Best leave Peter be for now." He turned again to Ezekiel. "We'll eat a bit late, after we see to all those who need keepin'." Gabriel looked up at the cold, blue sky. "God knows we all need a bit of keepin'," and he moved squarely off toward the muddied road.

Ezekiel didn't move, however; he just stayed near the church door, looking up at the opening sky. Like a bud, yes, like a bud it was opening in color and in glory. And Ezekiel spoke to the wind in low moans above its now barely audible whistle.

*   *   *

"Peter, don't you understand? Your son is dead! He's dead!"

Rachel was clutching herself, small and frail before him, but Peter did not move. He must not show weakness. Not now. His lips were tight and thin as he sat down in a chair, his face immobile. He spoke distinctly, staring at the wall before him.

"It's good I've found you down here. Don't go back up to that room. Don't ever go back into that room. I assume,

Elizabeth, that you've covered the body and closed the door. I'll see that a coffin is brought this afternoon and . . . ."

"But, Peter . . . ." Rachel's eyes were red. She was ugly and tired. He didn't want to look at her. Her face was repulsive to him, so streaked and dirty.

"Enough, Rachel!" Peter's voice was quick and peremptory. "You need sleep and a good deal of it. I never looked to see this happen, but now it has and he . . . it . . . the body must be out of the house. There will be many things to see to today, the coffin, the service, the grave, where—next to who. Marcus will be extra busy, too, what with all the people. . . ."

"God, Peter, stop, stop it. Do you hear?"

Rachel screamed at him, holding her hands fisted next to her mouth. Saliva dribbled onto them from her lips. Her nose ran, and Peter was disgusted by her obvious desperation, her weakness.

"Peter, he's your son, your last son—he's dead up there, dead—" Rachel struggled between huge sobs as Elizabeth ineffectually tried to comfort her. "Dead, Peter. And you, you haven't seen him in—in weeks." (She exaggerated, he thought, not weeks.) "God, g-good God, what are you afraid of that you won't even say good-goodbye to your own son? Go up there and look at him, Peter Wahab—and see that he's dead. Oh, God, that's all I ask. Do for him now what you would not do when he was alive. Oh, God! If you cannot look at him, if you cannot touch me—what will b-b-become of us, and what are we to do?"

Peter sat, silent and awful before his wife. He did not move. He dared not touch her—or any living thing. There was a long silence punctuated only by Rachel's broken sobs. Finally, he arose and moved toward the kitchen. He stopped at the door, turned, and said, "Elizabeth, my wife needs rest and care. Take her into the sitting room and lay her on the couch. Put a blanket over her to keep her warm while I make some coffee. I'll see Tom Aul about a coffin. Do not go up into that accursed room. Tom and the Wilson boys will see to it."

⚓ ⚓ ⚓

Ezekiel was moving up the beach, searching for his lost painting. He could not find it. His eyes moved over the wide expanse of sea, but (he knew) it was gone. The gulls were gathering swiftly along the shore, scavenging behind the storm, and Ezekiel realized that Ocracoke was only one of many islands set like jeweled prisons within the sea. He sang to himself as he walked—sang in answer to the sharp, shrill cry of the hungry birds.

⚓ ⚓ ⚓

*He that puts the crown to his
own use shall perish.*

Peter was adamant. He would not engage in such sentimental and shameless outbursts. It was to be expected of Rachel, a woman and a mother, but not of him. He did not understand why this had happened, but he would bear it without flinching. He would bear this injustice, this final indignity.

He walked swiftly through the mud, almost at a trot. He felt his boots slip at each step, and his thighs strained to keep the pace. Rachel had not been able to drink the coffee. Instead, she had cried even more and turned away from him, her face buried in the sofa, the two glass candelabra lamps, bought by Job in Virginia City long, long ago, tinkling against the shudder of her body. Even the small, stuffed shark, which he himself had inadvertently caught one day long ago while fishing the Stream miles out, had trembled slightly against the wall. It had been, Peter realized, the wind that made it do so.

Peter bowed his head. He was near Tom Aul's now, and

he trudged determinedly on. A cock crowed, late in the day but distinctly. Tom Aul kept a large yard of chickens, and Peter heard their faint commodious chatter as he turned from the road up the ragged, sand-filled pathway that led to Tom's work shed. The clouds moved over the buildings and earth in strange, undulating shadows. For a moment he felt the warmth of brilliant sunshine upon his back. The yard shimmered as he looked up from the path. Then the light moved across the stubble of grass, the chicken coop and yard, and into a cluster of live oak and yaupon that cut the back field in two. Peter shivered. His clothes clung damp and cold against his skin. The small gate creaked as he pushed through and stood briefly to watch the ever-increasing numbers of chickens now appearing in the yard.

"They'll brave the worst of weather, them will." Tom Aul's big voice greeted him from the door of the workshop. He was preparing to feed the chickens.

"Funny, ain't it? That cock crows like a real artist up there, and he's a good one, no doubt. But just hours ago he was shiverin' inside that coop with the rest of 'em. It's a wonder what a late feedin' will do for the most timid."

Tom cradled a small, rusted grain pail in his huge arm. His face was weathered and red, a full beard attempting to hide a long scar down the left side of his face from cheekbone to jaw. The scar was ugly and manifest. One could not avoid looking at it, and because Tom had gotten it late in years, it would never fade with the changes of a young man's skin.

"You usually don't stare so, Peter."

Peter looked quickly away toward the chickens. He hunched his shoulders and thrust his hands deep into his pockets. "I . . . ."

"I know why you've come, Peter. It's a small town on a small island. Bad news travels fast. It rides upon the wind, I think. Come walk my way a mite."

Tom opened the yard door and began broadcasting feed to

the multitude of chickens now in the enclosure. The action caused an even greater cacophony within the yard. "Never seen the chicken wasn't a bit peckish." Tom laughed momentarily at his own joke. "Always hungry, always brave, as long as they know I'm here to feed 'em. Now take that little rooster. A real tough one, he is. A bully, proud as a peacock most of the time. He rules the yard. His will is the law for these hens and chicks, yet he does as he pleases. Even used to come at me upon occasion. I look to see him do it again sometime, too, him and those red eyes o' his. Once I took him by his neck and wrung it good, wrung it until those little red beads o' his almost popped outa his head, and him all the while cacklin' like Satan himself and scratchin' at my gloves. Never flew at me again after that, nope, not for the longest time he didn't."

Peter stood inside the closed gate. He was annoyed by Tom's lack of understanding. Was this some crude allegory like that in the clouds, some awkward joke played upon him by a half-literate fisherman who knew only one foolish pun which he repeated over and over, year after year. Didn't Tom Aul really understand how painful this all was, these final acts? Peter could do nothing but stand and listen.

Finally, Tom finished his chores, and the two men walked slowly toward Aul's small house. Tom was more serious now, and he moved with the heavy, measured pace of a man who had learned through long years not to waste what energy was left him.

"Yes," he said as the two men reached the kitchen door, "those chickens love me, love me for the good I do 'em. Even the cock loves me, because I wrung his neck once. They're like the children of Israel, Peter, long-suffering in the desert of that yard for the promised fruit which I give 'em."

They sat down at the table for coffee, while Tom Aul continued to talk of chickens, of the unkempt look of the kitchen (for Ann was away at the hotel taking care of the shipwreck survivors), of the hook pulled out of a tarpon's mouth that had so scarred his face, of Joseph and Potiphar's wife, of the years of famine and the years of plenty, and of how good the seemingly harsh life of the islands really was.

As they drank, Peter understood. Tom Aul was afraid. Not knowing what to say, he could not stop talking, and afraid of saying the wrong thing, he spoke of anything at all. In growing disquietude, Tom Aul wanted to comfort him and was searching the air to do so.

"Tom, I wish a coffin for my son by day's end." Peter watched Aul finish swallowing coffee from a large, cracked ivory cup. The kitchen was dark and musty. It smelled of the rain and the winter. The silence was punctuated only by the click of Tom's cup as he placed it on the saucer in front of him and stared into the far corner of the room. There was no fire, and Tom drew a long breath, hugging his shoulders.

"It's ready, Peter. I have but to take it over, and Gabriel will come soon to help me with the chore." He looked across the table at Peter. "It's been a bad winter, friend. God, it's been a bad winter. We'll send to Morehead for a stone, soon's you give me a text to put on it. Lord, Peter, I don't know what to say."

"Then say nothing, man. Say nothing at all." Peter's eyes flinched. "I must be off about town and for home. What's done is done."

Peter pushed his chair away from the table and stood up. "I thank you for the coffee, Tom, but I must be about my business now."

"We'll take care of the arrangements, Peter," Tom said. "I'll get some boys down to the plot early mornin'. Don't you worry none. We'll do things right."

Peter left and walked toward the small, circular cove around which the town was built. He walked quickly and stayed for no one. Like his uncle before him, he would do what had to be done. The coffin and grave were attended to. He would choose the text for the stone that very night. The burial must be soon. It was best.

So it was that Job Wahab had closed his eyes and wept upon the day his brother died, wept passionately, without truly knowing why for some time (until young Peter came out of the charnel room), and then he stopped crying and grimly walked out of the house toward the low dunes across the island. The next day he oversaw the burial of Hosea in the family graveyard, and never, never while standing in the little copse protected by a tangle of live oak and yaupon, never did that same morose and bewildered look leave his face.

Peter saw Reverend Hawkins briefly at the town's only hotel, a reminder of those busy days of plenty when ships had anchored by the dozens off the outer bar and goods had flowed smoothly through the inlet in strong-ribbed ships to Elizabeth City, Washington, and New Bern. There he arranged for the service to be conducted on the following afternoon, Monday, at three o'clock. There would be a mercifully short period in the morning when people might call to express their sympathy.

Marcus said that at eight there was also to be a short service of thanks for those saved from the sea. The minister excused Peter from coming, but Peter assured him that Sunday was the Lord's day and both he and Rachel would present themselves in the family pew at the appointed hour.

From the hotel, Peter stopped at the church to recover his boots and oilskin. He made arrangements with Abigail Midgett for dinner to be carried to Rachel and Elizabeth. He was embarrassed when the woman assured him that she'd already seen to it.

Then, turning east across the island, Peter walked out of town toward the beach. The sand was still blowing hard from the northeast, but Peter wore no scarf. He walked over the purple muhly, stubbly and gray from the winter, past the waving cordgrass and brown sea oats until, topping the dunes, he saw the cold Atlantic stretching eastward to the horizon. Peter then turned north and walked steadily up the beach for almost an hour, never slowing and never looking up from the sand. Finally, he slipped, stopped, and stared blankly once again out to sea. For a long time he stood still, looking ahead, over the white-capped waves, feeling their spray, cold and wet against his face. But he saw no vision, no gift of knowledge from the empty sea, and so he turned sullenly away and walked across the dunes toward the Sound-side path and town. As he neared the path, however, Peter saw a holly bush. It was the same one from which he had broken a sprig for Rachel the day before.

"Oh, God," whispered Peter, stopping and staring at the bush, "you must not visit this upon me. What am I to do these long, lonely years without him, in this wide expanse of sea and upon this prison set within it? Where is my treasure now, set upon your mercy, and where is my heart? To whom will we call, and who will answer our loneliness?"

# IX

# THE FIERY CROSS

THE SERVICE was late Sunday. Unavoidably late, Gabriel Midgett felt, with all that had gone on that day. More was the pity. So many people would be tired and in no mood to come out on such a cold winter's evening. Nonetheless it was a good thing, the service. Men needed to pray every so often, needed to pray a lot. The outside world was always pulling a person apart, always asking of him and demanding something he either didn't have or couldn't do. Last night he thought they'd never save any of those people, much less every one of the thirty-seven men and women aboard. But they did save them and a miracle it was. A downright miracle for which Gabriel had no answer, only prayer. Things happened the way they did, and Gabriel had long ago decided it was foolishness to ask why.

The store sometimes wore on him and Abigail. It was extra work, and there were so many things to do the world could beat a man down. Like people clamoring for things the mail boat hadn't brought for a month and now most likely wouldn't bring for another. Like it must have beat Judith down before she up and left so many years ago. What a legend she was. Gabriel never really believed she'd run away out of fear of old Job. Why, she would've as soon blessed the old Pharaoh out as looked at him. She'd always laughed so much that even the niggers had liked her, though never as some people thought. She was a regular pilgrim, Gabriel thought. Judith had just not been an islander; to make anything more of it was foolishness. Gabriel chuckled. God save her!

Gabriel cleared his throat and looked toward the pulpit. The corners of the old coastguardsman's mouth rose, and he shook his head. A body should never be too good.... Of what use were legends after all?

Peter and Rachel Wahab were sitting stock upright in the family pew. Rachel had a fine, smooth curve to her back even now, even after all these years and pregnancies. And it must be hard living with Peter Wahab, a man who—like now—could never get up off his knees. Peter kneeling. Should've known he couldn't sit for long.

For a minute Gabriel imagined he saw Pharaoh there, hard on his knees too, praying in barely audible, sharp monosyllables, twisting his bristled and taut face with every word, over and over and over.

How it must have hurt the old man when Judith, in a fit for not being allowed an outing to Morehead City, had dumped a consignment of tea off the dock. She'd stood there, her back straight and taut, her pert, tiny breasts bold with her youth and the exhilaration of her defiance. But old Pharaoh had known how to calm God's own storms. Standing in the doorway which his daughter had so precipitously flung open, his face hard with the inevitability of his daughter's rebellion, he had said, "Thank you, good daughter. We shall drink yaupon."

She had stood dumb before him. Her sodden rebellion had floated heavily upon the water, slowly coloring the sea a light rust. Then, painfully disintegrating, it had sunk to the bottom or floated out with the tide. Then she'd spit in the water and walked away. Gabriel chuckled in spite of himself. Oh Lord— to be like her, to have that kind of spirit.

Gabriel turned in the doorway and began ushering the incoming people to their seats. Strangers all, but he knew that, unlike Peter and Rachel Wahab, the thirty-seven survivors of the dismembered ship would most certainly all come to thank God that they had been spared. There was no answer for such disparity. Gabriel knew, too, that there was no feeling sorry for Peter and Rachel. The loss was beyond that. One could only build upon the debris, hold fast and build anew each year. He ushered Marty Terrell to her seat and rubbed his hands briskly as he walked back toward the door.

Gabriel himself was that kind of man. He held fast to things, not the temporal things that he felt so often deluded his neighbors, not the houses and barns, the horses and livestock, the clothes and furniture and knickknacks and trifles. No, Gabriel Midgett was wiser, more cleverly homiletic than his neighbors. The store was just a building to him, a warehouse. Master of the station was his way in the world. He and Abigail could get along without the store. He ran it for profit, rightful gain, but the men at the station were more central to his life. The store helped his neighbors; Midgett felt the unity of the village folk to be a stark necessity on the island, so he'd gone in with Peter when everyone thought the store done for. He would always order any necessities the townsfolk wished from Morehead City or Greenville, even as far away as Raleigh, no matter how few items were required; but such things had to be paid for. The store never made much of a profit, but it always made enough.

Yes, Gabriel Midgett was a man of the flesh and of the sea, sinful beyond hope, yet called to do the Lord's bidding. He put his trust in things of substance and moment: the steadfast structures of human contact. He liked people. That was why the store had been a success these last years. Folks trusted the Midgetts. Gabriel would always do what he could for you. He had a firm hand and an attentive ear. If you needed something from the mainland, the Midgetts would get it for you, sure 'nough. Not that he wouldn't drive a hard bargain. No one ever scaled Gabriel Midgett clean. Gabriel was a man you could put your faith in. A good captain, he was hard bedrock, stable and solid. A good leader to the boys at the station.

"To be a pilgrim," they were singing, and Gabriel moved to his accustomed seat in the last pew near the closed doors. It was a large crowd. You could hardly hear the wind above the singing and the low, constant roar of a winter's sea on a clear, cold, silent night, the ocean peaceful but never senescent. Such seeming moderation was always fugitive.

Gabriel shifted his weight uneasily as he sat in the pew. It was to be a night of singing and thanks. For him, these were difficult meetings. He'd torn the tendons along the back of his leg right severely some years back, and it was actin' up.

Last night hadn't been good. All this standing and sitting would hardly make things better. He watched Peter Wahab's immobile face as the congregation began the second hymn. His friend's body never moved. Tall and thin, he betrayed himself only in the tiredness of his slightly hunched shoulders. Even then, thought Gabriel, it really wasn't that the shoulders drooped, for Peter was making an effort to stand ramrod straight. It was that Wahab's head bent slightly lower. What? Why, Peter was actually looking at the hymnal, reading words he'd memorized years ago. That was the difference. Peter always prided himself on his memory, his ability (and it really was a delight to old Job as well) to "sing the hymnal with nary a second look." Yet, here was Peter Wahab staring at the hymnal but singing words by rote.

"Worn out," Gabriel said aloud to himself without realizing it.

*Rock of Ages, cleft for me . . . .*

The singing continued louder, a rhythmic weariness disciplining the congregation.

*Should my tears forever flow,*
*Should my zeal no respite know?*

The hymn's mystique invaded every corner of the church.

*Thou must save and Thou alone.*

Yes, that had happened. Thirty-seven people should have died last night abreast of the shore, yet they had not. All were alive and passably well off right here in the church. Beside such awesome miracles, all else fell to insignificance. The Lord had saved so many. Who could blame folks if they counted numbers?

*While I draw this fleeting breath,*
*When mine eyelids close in death . . . .*

Marcus Hawkins had chosen this hymn for Peter and Rachel Wahab, but lost in its sensuous abasement, few assembled understood its more subtle impropriety. They sang because all singing was joy, and joy itself was a last refuge and safeguard.

> *When I soar to worlds unknown,*
> *And behold Thee on thy throne,*
> *Rock of Ages, cleft for me,*
> *Let me hide myself in Thee.*

The singing stopped and the congregation sat down, tired but happy in their ignorance, glad for a rest well won, for a quiet time in which to drowse and be instructed. The sermon would be short, its message predictable, and the comfort of home and sleep welcome. Only Peter Wahab, seated and slumped forward in his pew, continued to stare at the open pages of the hymnal before him.

"Greetings to you all, good Christians, and as Paul said to the Galatians, 'Grace be to you and peace from God the Father, and from our Lord Jesus Christ.' Amen." A sympathetic murmur passed through the church as the Reverend Marcus Hawkins rose to the pulpit.

"And tonight, brothers and sisters, I wish to take as my text Paul's letter to those same people who had so early forgotten the Lord, forgotten his real ways and forgotten how to live beneath both his judgment and his mercy."

Marcus Hawkins looked up briefly from his text toward Peter.

"Remember, Paul says in Galatians 2:16:

> *Knowing that a man is not justified*
> *by the works of the law, but by the*
> *faith of Jesus Christ, even we have*
> *believed in Jesus Christ, that we*
> *might be justified by the faith of*
> *Christ, and not by the works of the*

*law: for by the works of the law
shall no flesh be justified.*

Marcus sighed, waited, and stared at the ceiling. He began again.

"Brethren, there are many here who were saved last night from the darkness and the hell of a cold, wet grave, saved by those of our men who braved the sea and its dangers to bring them in. It would have been horrible beyond measure had they all died out there, each one desperately clinging to the torn pieces of planking and timber that the sea might hopelessly have offered them in their fear and ignorance, each man and woman desperate for life, gasping for even a moment's breath, terrified and shivering at the imminence of that very death which we all must surely undergo before we meet our Lord. But it was not to be."

Reverend Hawkins acknowledged a collective murmur and a staccato of amens.

"Gabriel Midgett and his brave men worked through the night to bring the survivors ashore, those very survivors who are with us tonight, beside you in the pews. After failure upon failure, seven tries in all, a line was shot out to the remains of the ship, and Gabriel Midgett himself, with no fear for his own life, went out to the ship on the line and helped send all those lost and stranded souls ashore. And now we are here. By God's will we are all here tonight—to give thanks—to express our joy for the Lord's great mercy. Our faith has been justified. So many among us have been spared."

There was another murmur of approval. Marcus glanced at Peter, still face down in his pew.

"But what if they had all died?

"I do not mean to wish it, forgive me, but what if such a thing had happened? Would it have made any difference in God's plan? We would have asked, 'Why? Why should such a terrible thing happen? Why should so many die? Why?'

"And in truth we would have received no obvious answer. We are only human and cannot ever here know God's great plan for his creation. We are not justified ever by the law, for we can never know it perfectly. The old law of sin and retribution is inadequate for both our joy and our sorrow. It has long since gone.

"Why? 'Why' we would have asked, and there would have been only silence, the whisper of the wind and the roar of the sea. Silence.

*But if we live by the law,*
*we shall die by it.*

"Yet these people did not die. Paul continues, 'If righteousness come by the law, then Christ is dead in vain. . . . Received ye the Spirit by the works of the law or by the hearing of faith?' he asks later. Brethren, I tell you here tonight that we must live by mighty acts of faith if we are to live truly in Christ. No law will make us live or tot up our debts and dues. No law will give us miracles. No man will find his way through this world except by faith and faith alone. And no faith ever was that was proved true by acts.

"Faith is. It would not have mattered a whit if all of us, Gabriel and his crew, all of us here in the church tonight, had been drowned by a great tidal wave from the sea. We have lived with such dangers all our lives, and death itself would have been a miracle of equal proportions. Faith is!

" 'Christ came in the fullness of time to redeem them that were under the law.' Paul promised us that. Yesterday we were huddled together against the ferocity of the storm. We closed our eyes in the fastness of our own souls and prayed for mercy. The clouds darkened the sky. Rain and wind beat against our homes, and under the curse of the law, we could not see. Brethren, when you leave this church tonight, look around you. There are multitudes of stars in a cold, blue heaven. Winter will pass away to spring and spring once more to summer. It is given us to suffer, only that we may know God the better for it. Stand fast!

> *Stand fast therefore in the liberty*
> *wherewith Christ has made us free....*
> *Walk in the Spirit.*

"I say to you tonight, no man is free until he is truly humbled before God's terrible love. No man is truly free but that he is in bondage to faith—faith born out of sin and fear, faith forged in the fires of loneliness and lust, but faith always ready to bear the fruit of eternal love, the great tyranny by which God rules our lives—eternal love—love that renders us free from the subtle greed and pride of our own spirit. We can make no more bargains with God, bargains that leave us only men, shut out of heaven itself. If we had all died, it would have been because God loved us.

"For every man must bear his own burden— of joy or grief. 'Lord, I believe,' saith the sinner. 'Help me in my unbelief.' We live in faith, brethren, and even faith itself, that mighty rock upon which God lifts us up out of the deepness of our unworthiness, even faith itself is in bondage to the unknown goodness and love which is God's mysterious mercy.

"We cannot, we must not, contest against it.

> *In due season, we shall*
> *reap, if we faint not.*

Oh, friends, faint not, and be humble, obedient in faith. For only then can we be finally and triumphantly free—in that liberty that is Christ's."

The sermon ended and the piano began the closing hymns. Gabriel rose stiffly from his seat. Marcus's sermons were always a mite stuffy, and this was no exception; but the minister was always sensible and pious when he dealt with folk.

Gabriel liked that. It was his final test of a good minister. If Marcus Hawkins never lived up to the promise of his sermons, he also never demanded the strict adherence of his flock to their prohibitions. The eminent practicality of this presented itself forcefully before Gabriel Midgett. The good minister gave a hard and rough community of islanders and seamen a conscience. And that was certainly useful. Such a rule of life, no questions asked, had purpose and effect.

This kind of sermon, however, asked far more from a man than just obedience and propriety. It hinted at an intimate and intense knowledge which Gabriel at once knew was inimical to good social order and conformity of action (which above all protected a man from the enormities of his own capricious will). Such structures were the responsibilities of neighbor to neighbor and the duty of man to God. They were stable and knowable. A man could follow such rules.

To "feel" God was another thing entirely, and this was what the minister had spoken of while the seaman attempted assiduously to avoid it with all his soul. Many townsfolk knew this intimacy with their Maker, the awfulness of palpable divinity, but to Gabriel it was a frightening abstraction suggesting too much the changeableness of human desire. What was that hymn, the tune of which he liked so much?

*Love divine, all love excelling . . . .*

That was it, but the idea was so hard to grasp.

Gabriel Midgett was uncomfortable with so fickle and transient a world. The outside world pulled on you, and tiring though it was, it was best to meet those demands, to do your duty. God gave man a rule and man obeyed it. That was goodness. The theologic complexities of faith, love, freedom, and personal revelation were beyond Gabriel by choice. He gloried in the loss of self that action brought him, the life at the station, Abigail, the children around the village, even the additional responsibility of the store. These were the strong lines with which Gabriel anchored his life, and he rarely looked upward.

Thus, Gabriel left the church generally satisfied—though discontented and somewhat disturbed by the sermon. It was the unease that made him turn (turn perversely, it seemed) away from town and walk quickly with long, strong steps toward the east shore. He walked the beach for almost fifteen minutes after he arrived there, not fully knowing why but peering into the dark, gray sky. A few, last gulls circled overhead, and a solitary sandpiper still searched the long reaches of the beach. There was nothing else. Then Gabriel turned homeward, leaving the lonely sand and sea to the enveloping night. He felt the need of people around him, laughing and eating, at least talking to one another, and even his worry over Peter Wahab's loss, which weighed heavily upon his mind, could not keep him any longer to himself.

At the church, people left slowly by twos and fours, stopping to talk to one another as they did so, forming small groups by the steps, chatting in low, respectful voices before moving on. Some walked up front to give sympathy to Rachel or to just nod their heads, clasping Rachel's hands in silent, inarticulate sorrow and then leaving. His friends of many years, Peter ignored them all. Neighbors of his family for generations passed in front of him shadowlike as he stood immobile in his pew, staring at the altar, the open hymnal lying upon his crooked fingers. The congregation had sung two final hymns. Peter repeated them over and over with unspeaking lips:

> *Abide with me; fast falls the eventide;*
> *The darkness deepens; Lord, with me abide.*

The words were worn and uncomforting to him now as the shadows filed past, one by one. The darkness of the church deepened as the candles were extinguished. Peter repeated a final phrase to himself, turning it over and over in his mind.

*Throw down your cross*
*Throw down your cross*

Why were these people bothering him so?

"I hope the sermon was of some comfort, Peter."

It was Marcus Hawkins's voice, far away near Rachel. Why did they all crowd in upon him? The sermon had been a tragic mistake. He had never finished it. Why did they remind him of it so? He had never finished it.

*All my life I grew up among sages*
*and have found nothing better*
*for anyone than silence.*

Peter looked down at the open book in his hands.

*Throw down your cross.*

What did it mean?

*Greater is learning than*
*priesthood or royalty.*

But that was not so. Squinting, he peered toward the altar.

*Throw down your cross.*

The church was partitioned by darkness. The altar was dim and unfathomable before him. Slowly, Peter put down his hymnal and rose from his seat in the pew. He pushed past Rachel and Marcus into the aisle and walked toward the altar. Almost no one was in the church now, and only Marcus and Rachel watched the lone, tall man walk up to the altar, grasp the standing cross with one hand, lift it to eye level, and remain holding it there for long minutes.

Rachel held her breath in short, staccato gasps.

Marcus was aghast. The minister looked around but saw no one and did not know what to do, so he remained still, never moving from where he stood. It was sacrilege, he thought, the way Peter looked. Something momentous was about to happen. Would Peter fall on his knees, or throw down the cross, or cry to heaven in his despair? Of what use had been the sermon if this was to occur?

But nothing happened. Peter remained staring at the cross, his arms eventually beginning to tremble with the strain, and finally he slowly lowered it to the altar once more. Rachel wept. Her husband turned and walked down the steps, seeing Rachel and Marcus as if for the first time. He stopped in front of them.

"Come, wife," he said, looking at Rachel directly, his eyes tired and his face drawn in intense lethargy. "Come, I can walk this way no longer."

Rachel glanced helplessly at Marcus and then rose and silently left the church.

After a while, Marcus Hawkins stopped gazing out of the open door. He turned and went about his business of closing up the building and getting home before the cold winter air gave him a chill. He peered at the stricken cross only briefly before he left.

# X

# PROPHETS I

IT WAS EARLY Monday morning when Peter rose, washed himself in cold water that had sat too long on the bed stand, dressed, and went downstairs. Rachel was up. She had risen, even earlier than was her custom, from a restless sleep, put on her robe, and gone downstairs. For hours Peter had listened to her moving and working in the rooms below. Elizabeth was no longer in the house, so Rachel worked alone, with the sharp, measured sounds of a person alone and grimly purposeful. Peter entered the kitchen, walked to the cupboard, and took out his coffee mug.

Rachel, cleaning on the back porch when he entered the kitchen, turned quickly to look at him. "You gave me a start."

"Oh, I'm sorry for it. I'll have my coffee now and help you in a bit," he replied. Peter then walked over to the stove and poured himself a large cup of steaming coffee.

It was a clear day, cloudless and sunlit and cold. He walked to the fireplace and put his back to the warm, open flames. For a long time he remained silent, feeling the sharp, satisfying prick of the heat against his calves and buttocks. He watched the brown-tipped yucca bend and shift erratically in the morning breeze. His free hand played aimlessly with his nose and mouth.

"You did well to make a fire, Rachel. The stove would not have kept us warm on a morning such as this."

Rachel looked up from her work, then put it aside and came into the kitchen. "It has been morning for a long while, Peter. The sun has been up some three hours now, and it will soon be time for dinner."

Peter gripped his cup tightly. He had not thought he'd slept so long.

"You were tired, Peter, very tired, and I left you asleep because you seemed to need it so much."

Rachel stopped, held her breath, then began once more, her stubby fingers peeling cracked paint away from a fissure in the tabletop.

"The coffin is at church now. Tom was over earlier in the morning to tell me. Marcus has arranged for the service. It'll be at three o'clock this afternoon."

> *The generations shall come of
> your children that shall rise
> up after you, and the strangers
> that come from afar shall say
> when they see the sickness and
> plague of the land....*

"I'm sorry about the way I acted . . . ." Peter put his cup down and looked away into the fireplace.

"No, Peter." Rachel rose from the table and moved to him. She put her hand upon his and drew it down from his face to her breast.

"You acted as any man might. Any man who has lost four children within a season of God's wisdom. Don't do this to yourself. We must stand together now; more than ever now God has given us each other, and our sons will never know the infirmities and sadness of age. You are a fine man, Peter." She gripped his hand harder, knelt down, and put her head against his chest, enfolding herself within him like a small, frightened girl. Peter looked at the empty cup on the table and embraced her tightly. He was so tired, so very, very tired.

> *See, I have set before thee
> this day life and good, and
> death and evil....*

"I don't understand, Rachel."

"It is not for us to understand, Peter."

He felt the moist warmth of her breath. She was almost begging, he thought, and what had he to give? He looked at the walls. The mortar needed painting in this old house. He had not touched it for a long while now. The very stone walls of the cottage, rare stone, not timber, brought to the island from so far away, built so long ago at such great cost, those walls were his to mend. He had not been a good husbandman these many years.

There was a loud banging on the door and Peter blinked as if from sleep. Rachel turned in his arms and pulled from him, wiping her eyes with her apron as she did so.

"Oh, it must be Gabriel, Peter. Tom said he'd be over late this morning. Oh, and look at me. I must be a sight." She hurried into the hallway. "Will you get the door, Peter? I'll go upstairs and dress. We'll have a bite to eat in a while. Don't forget to ask Gabriel to stay."

"Yes, yes, I'll do that. Go on about things," Peter called back mechanically. He went to the front door, opened it, and ushered Gabriel Midgett into the sitting room.

For a while, the two men could only exchange greetings. The weather seemed better. Yes, it would hold steady for a spell, surely. Big storms often brought an early spring. It was certainly needed. And Job's palmetto had taken a turn for the worse. Peter meant to cut it down one of these days. Fishing should be good after the storm. Another ship was lost off Cape Lookout night before last, all seventeen hands down with her.

Lookout, it was perhaps the only cape in the Atlantic almost as much feared as Hatteras. Certainly it had been unlucky this time.

Gabriel shifted his feet, pushing them awkwardly under the front of the sofa every so often and then leaning back, his arms spread away from him. Soon the discomfort would force him forward, and he would push his feet into the center of the room and lean down to rub them. Peter rested his elbows on the worn arms of his chair, pulling on his nose and avoiding his friend's eyes.

"Peter," Gabriel finally said, "I have come to talk of other things— I am sorry for all that has happened, Peter—I must say that."

"I know you are, Gabriel." Peter dreaded the next minutes. His right hand fumbled with a doily. "But what be these other things of which you speak?"

"Don't put me off, Peter," Gabriel charged. "We're too good friends for that. I've spoken to Marcus Hawkins this morning."

"Yes."

"He told me of last night."

"And do you wish to speak of it?"

"I do."

"Then who am I to stop you, my friend? I have no more to say than I said last night. No more, no less. I am tired, Gabriel, and can do no more in this."

"I've not been your friend for months, Peter Wahab. You haven't let me. And it is not yours to decide." Gabriel was almost peremptory. It was only his compassion and humility of person that allowed him to speak so, and he forced Peter to listen.

"It is not yours to say, not yours to decide what must be done. Peter, I walked for a long while last night on the beach. It must have been about the same time you and Rachel were with Marcus." Gabriel paused, as if to give Peter time for reflection. He looked out the window, then back at Peter. "I was worried for you, Peter, for the two of you. It's not easy, a terrible thing such as you've suffered, Lord knows. But you must not let it do this to you. You must not." He hurried on now, almost abashed at what he was saying, confused and disarmed by Peter's silence.

"I walked a long time on that sand, at least it seemed so. And do you know what kept goin' over and over in my mind? It was that saying on old Sarah Meekins's tombstone. Do you remember it, Peter?

> *Oh, I must go down to the sea once more*
> *To the open sand and the sea*

*And all I ask is a tall, tall ship
And my God to be with me.*

It's a foolish ditty, Peter, but it kept going over and over in my mind."

"Do you mean, Gabriel, that I ask too much? I've lost four sons, Gabriel. Four sons! What is little enough to ask? I no longer wish a tall ship. It was long ago my ancestor came here upon one. I'm an islander now, captive of the sea; not upon it, but within it. Is one of four sons left to me too much to ask?" Peter whispered the words, not speaking to Gabriel but grimly staring beyond him over miles and years.

Gabriel was reticent. He felt himself presumptuous and ungraceful beside his friend's formality, but he continued.

"Yes, Peter, if you've none left you." He would not compromise with this man, Gabriel thought. Peter Wahab must see and accept the truth.

"Ah, Peter, we've been friends too long, and I'm no one to lecture the likes of you; but that's what I mean. Out there on the beach, it was clear to me that nothing is too much to ask; wish for the world if you want. Nothing is too much to ask if only it's possible, if only it's before us. But the Lord cannot and will not give you what He's already taken away, and you mustn't wish for it, Peter. It is a sin and presumption before the Almighty. The boys are gone. Don't weep too much or too little. Your courage has always had a little and more of pride in it, Peter. Justified, to be sure; you're a smart and educated man. We all know and respect that, but you cannot bargain with God, Peter."

"People have bargained with Him before. Noah, Moses. He made a covenant with Israel." Peter's whisper was hollow, on the edge of anger, but Gabriel would not stop.

"They made no vain pact, Peter. The old laws of Israel gave us only hell as a resting place.

"Lord, Peter." Gabriel leaned forward and held his friend hard by the wrist. "Don't contend so. I see it tearin' at you to do it. You've never lived in this world, Peter, not our world, where folks like me are. You've always been off on your mountain. You've always had more and always wanted less. You've given up more than I'll ever make, and still you've been left with Job's treasures. Your house was built with Pharaoh's stone, and you've filled it with his wealth."

Gabriel stopped short. He had caught himself in something that seemed to him dangerously close to open envy displayed at the most inappropriate of times. He was ashamed.

"And what else would you have me do, Gabriel, give up this house and turn my wife naked out into the world?" Peter wanted his sarcasm to hurt. He was enraged that this man would speak to him so, at this moment, when so little was left.

"Peter, Peter, I've no children, but I must be grateful—" There was a long pause. The hallway clock whirred and chimed the hour. Gabriel shook his head and looked at the floor.

"No, Peter, I do not want you to give up any more."

Peter remained rigid in his chair, watching Gabriel intently while his friend hunched over and stared at the carpeted floor.

"But you must know, Peter, that no man may buy God, not his justice, not his mercy. Such as these are freely given, and we must find them where we can. Here on the island we've only ourselves, and if we don't have God's mercy, then we must accept his justice. Don't ask why, Peter. Why don't do no good. Why do those yuccas all around your house have spines so sharp they'll pierce a man's hand, yet every summer God's candle rises straight and six feet tall out of the middle of 'em? I don't know. Why did Pharaoh ever kill that nigger? Because he practiced witchcraft like some people say? I don't know. Judith might have, but she's gone and won't ever come back; and we've got to live with what's left us."

Gabriel stopped. He was sweating and his face was drawn and taut. He didn't lift his head. He'd taken too many liberties, he felt, and he was afraid he'd done his friend no good. Yet he feared for this man, feared for him if he would not listen.

Peter stared for a second at the wall. Then he looked out at Pharaoh's tree. The witchcraft story was little known in the town, and even the few who knew of it paid it little mind. Had Judith been interested in witchcraft? Was that why Pharaoh had beaten the man to death? Was that why Judith had left? Was she cast out by Job in his anger to wander and die alone in a foreign land? Peter rubbed his eyes with the fingers of one hand and brought it down over his face. The idea was too absurd to contemplate. What was all Job's praying for if not to.... Peter didn't know. He fumbled with his large hands as they lay on his knees.

"It's hard to believe, Gabriel," he said, "that Job ever did that. He was a good and pious man. I used to watch him at church or praying sometimes with us at night, and I always wanted to be like him, God-fearing, upright, always walking amongst my neighbors earnestly and doing good. Why? Why, Gabriel, must this visitation come again and again? For a long time I could not accept this final chastening, this—"

Peter shook his head from side to side and looked at Gabriel. "Gabriel, for the longest time yesterday, all the way home from church and even after I'd come home and then left for Tom Aul's, I didn't believe it. I didn't believe it was possible for God so to punish me. I walked believing that Isaac would live again, that I would see him walking toward me on the path, young and healthy like before, smiling through the rain. I didn't believe he was dead, Gabriel. I was sure he was alive, just waiting for me to find him, like we played hide-and-seek so long ago, and when I couldn't find him, he'd holler from the closet or in back of the couch, 'You haven't looked here, Daddy.' And I'd look and he'd be there, smiling and laughing at me. He'd be there."

The room darkened as sunlight bent toward the eastern wall, played freakishly across the plates and knickknacks, and then skittered into the hallway. The house seemed to Gabriel fanciful, almost frivolous. He had never seen it like this before.

"But, Peter." Gabriel's hands on his shoulders were heavy and rude. "Your son is dead. How could you know it unless you saw him so? For some people only God's will is needed, but He's always had to show you. You should have looked upon your son to see that he had left you. You're a hard man, Peter. Rachel needs you now. It's in your bones, this stubbornness, and while it makes you mighty, it makes you hard. You've neither been punished nor rewarded, Peter. You're only human."

Peter made no reply. The man's hands were so oppressive, so heavy and strong upon his shoulders. Human, why of course he was human. He'd never questioned that, had he? Wasn't that why he gave up Job's wealth, to prove it, to insist upon it? What did all these years mean if not that he was human?

Rachel walked into the room and broke the spell. Gabriel stood up to greet her. They must go to church, she said. The services would begin in an hour and a half, and they must eat quickly if they were to get there before folks started arriving to pay their last respects. The soup was hot and Gabriel would take a bite with them before seeing his wife to church.

Peter followed the two into the dining room and sat quietly while Rachel put out the good china and went into the kitchen to get soup, bread, and milk. The three ate in a silence broken only by the brief, self-conscious rattle of Rachel's nervous chatter. Neither man wanted to speak of what had passed between them. Some precious and delicate treasure had been broken, smashed beyond all hope of repair, yet neither man wanted to pick up the pieces and throw them away. So they averted their eyes and remembered what used to be. The afternoon shadows fell onto the white linen tablecloth through the two small windows. The three sipped their soup. Peter thought Gabriel's manners loud and vulgar and wondered why he hadn't realized it before.

Rachel looked from one man to the other and slowly stopped talking herself. Something had happened. Rachel had been taught to hold tight. Like any islander, she prided herself on her stoicism under suffering, but now she was on the raw edge of her loneliness. As she watched the two men finish their soup, Rachel prayed God for help.

They would find their way within all this, she thought. Folks are not alone forever, thank God, and Peter must come to her. She wiped her hands on her napkin and pushed her chair back to begin gathering the dishes.

"You men go put on your coats now, and I'll be with you shortly," she said. "I'll just stack the dishes. Peter, your boots are on the back porch. I cleaned them this morning. Help Gabriel with his coat."

Gabriel was already moving toward the hall, but Peter was still sitting at the table. He rose stiffly, his face impassive.

"You hurry, Rachel. I'll stack the dishes."

"What's that, Peter?" Rachel called from the kitchen.

"I said you go now. I'll be staying home."

Rachel twisted her head toward him in disbelief.

"No, Peter!"

"You need not worry. Go with Gabriel and I shall be here when you return. Make no apologies for me. I wish no inconvenience to anyone."

"No, Peter!"

Gabriel returned from the hallway and squinted incredulously at Peter.

"My God, man, go! Stand beside your wife," he begged.

After a long pause, Peter answered.

"I will not visit that grave, Gabriel. Ever!"

Gabriel held Rachel's wrap on his arm. He went to her and put it upon her shoulders. "Come, Rachel, we'll be late. Your husband needs this time alone. We'll go to church together."

"Yes—yes, I-I'll be coming, Gabriel." Rachel spoke woodenly, in disbelief. "We'll be home soon, Peter. You—you wait for us now, you hear."

Gabriel hurried Rachel out the door, and Peter heard the wind slam it shut behind them. The house was empty now. The big man sighed and closed his eyes; then he rose from the table, still gripping an unused spoon from the silver service.

He crossed the room and walked into the hall. Stopping beside the stairs, however, and looking up into the darkness, he saw the door to Isaac's room swing open and a bright shaft of light flood down the stairs. The windows were open. Rachel must have been airing the room and neglected to shut the door tightly. It would be getting on toward late afternoon by the time Rachel and Gabriel returned. The light momentarily dazzled Peter, and he shut his eyes. He had told Rachel never to go into that room. Peter looked away at the plate on the wall, then at the spoon that he held in his hand. Unmoving, he contemplated it a long while. Finally a smile, possibly mixed with contempt, flickered across his face. He placed the spoon on the hall table and walked doggedly up the stairs. The windows had to be closed. Night would be coming on, a cold, clear winter's night.

# XI

# PROPHETS II

EZEKIEL PLAYED by the shore. At least to anyone looking at him it would have seemed play. Actually, it wasn't, not to old Ezekiel. He was building again. The onshore winds had fitfully picked up toward noon, and he had not been able to keep his castle solid. The sands dried out too quickly in such weather, and each time Ezekiel built his stronghold, tall and turreted like the ones he'd seen along the river in Miz Midgett's picture book years back, it would crumble and fall before the gusting breeze. By now he had only shapeless mounds of sand around him, and he was tired of trying.

He threw a handful of sand toward the sea and grimaced as the wind cast it back, stinging, in his face. He knew that he should be at Isaac's funeral, but something kept him from it. He was not afraid of Peter. He had immediately forgiven the white man his sins. It was part of the visitation, God's curse upon the islands, that Peter Wahab should act so. He was also sure that Wahab himself would not be at the church service, and Ezekiel was strongly tempted to go to the cottage and see the old man. But that would not do.

"They neva lissen to me," he whispered to the wind. "They neva lissen to ole Zeke. But I know. God, oh God, He wants his people free— He wants to set 'em free and that was neva done wiffout sufferin', a whole lot of sufferin'. Set my people free. Lord, we knows, don' we?"

Ezekiel's voice changed with the direct address, and suddenly the old Negro sat himself down upon the dry, blowing sand and started singing to himself, all the while intently inspecting a painting that he had made earlier in the morning, which now, its outlines blurred by the film of sand adhering to its still-wet surface, shimmered in the afternoon light.

"Let my people go," Ezekiel chanted. The dark blues at the top of the canvas caught his eye again. He loved them so. They were as deep as the ocean, like an evening sky fading into night. Along the left side a huge, malevolent, black funnel dominated the length of the painting. Like death itself, the funnel was grotesque, fantastic, purposeful, and it widened to fill the canvas as it mounted toward the blue. At its edges the funnel transmuted into protean masses of grim clouds rising precipitously across the skies. Veering first this way, then that, the clouds folded in upon themselves only to shift and modify themselves anew in another area of the painting.

Amidst this tumult, barely visible and constantly taking upon itself the diverse and preternatural hues of the skies, was an immense and discontinuous city. Shadowed as if by a storm, its spires broke capriciously out of the clouds and wove themselves again into the sky's strange, eccentric texture. Great gilded roadways, red and blue under a monstrous sun which shed its light into and through the upper reaches of the funnel, swept precariously through the lower half of the painting, sometimes connecting buildings, sometimes disappearing into the turmoil around them. Ezekiel sat entranced by his creation, as if he could not or would not believe it his own.

He knew that the painting was not yet finished. There were eddies here and there, areas where the tenuous balance of lines and colors lost significance. Invariably the phantasms became muddied and dull in places like this. Ezekiel's fingers ran without friction over the canvas to its lower, left-hand corner and forced brusquely upward the lines of a small pustule of red, oily paint. No, the painting was not yet finished, but it could not be left here or brought back to the Midgetts'. This painting was not the wind's as so many others had been. The old man's wizened face squinted in a cruel grin as he inspected a small, sticklike figure, almost unnoticeable by any eye other than his own, which cowered at the base of a tall monument that jutted skyward in wanton arrogance to engage the mountainous clouds.

To anyone else, the whole painting might have seemed an hallucination of some great and final catastrophe. Nemesis moved through the urgently gathering and ungathering clouds, unseen but persistent, adamant, resistless in his power. Few would have guessed with what great care and craft Ezekiel had structured the painting. To an islander, the canvas would have seemed merely another mess, one of those foolish wastes of time and effort that the old darky often created when he wasn't "just right." Actually, the old man could do better, much better, when he'd a mind to. They would have passed it off as such.

But Ezekiel knew better. It was an exact rendering, an imitation of his vision, of the previous night's storm, and of his dream: their fury, their magnificence, their annunciation. Ezekiel trembled at the thought of it, the storm, the shuddering boards and timbers of the shed, the cold, wet water spraying in upon him, the terrific sound that the sky and wind had made.

It had been like that for three days when they had come over on the great ship years ago. His mother had told him many, many times how thirty-three souls died in the ship's hold, drowned praying to their gods, and thirty-three more were thrown overboard to save the ship from sinking. It was a story older than Ezekiel, told from mother to child through generations. He remembered, too, how the fire came out of the sky after three days to still the waters and bring a great thirst to all on board, how many more died until skeletons were left where men and women had once been, and how babies died sucking dry and shriveled breasts.

Ezekiel knew that his grandmother, one of the Seven Sisters, had been horribly disfigured by the sickness that the white men brought her. And he knew, finally, that no one could go back again. The garden of peace and plenty was lost forever so that men had to work out their sins upon earth amidst great toil and suffering, unable to know why God did what He did. Deborah had told him all this and he remembered.

Then, Ezekiel turned to his sack and instruments still strewn upon the ground near the fallen sand castle. He quickly gathered up his belongings and put them in the sack, slinging the torn and shredded canvas roughly over his back and about his shoulder like a crude knapsack. He turned back again to the painting and carefully picked it up so that only the back of the canvas touched the front of his body and stomach. Like this, he began an arduous and clumsy jog trot north along the beach. His knees kept hitting the bottom of the canvas stretcher. Ezekiel was afraid of falling and spoiling the painting, so he slowed to a gull-like waddle, carefully maintaining his balance, ever mindful of the precious and incomplete vision that he carried with him.

The spot for which Ezekiel headed was five miles up the beach and two hundred yards inland, alongside a short, tidal stream that nearly bisected the island and was known as Basin Creek. It was a favorite haunt of the old Negro; and it was here, safely guarded by the enveloping myrtles and black locust, that Ezekiel, as of late, took all his most important work. He would finish the painting there, he thought, finish it and let it dry. For now, Ezekiel knew the meaning of the awful winter's storm and what it heralded. He knew now (actually he didn't know like other people, he thought to himself, like white folks or even normal black men) why Peter Wahab's children had been taken from him. Ezekiel was aware of what to do with his painting now, and as he stumbled along the cold, wet beach, he could hear Deborah's voice, at first crooning softly to him but soon singing loudly and triumphantly the old gospel rhythms which he knew so well.

# XII

# THE MOURNING

ALL THE TOWNSPEOPLE were at the funeral service. Creekers and Pointers both, Rachel thought, as she watched from down the road as family after family entered the church before her. She was glad for Gabriel's strong arm next to her. It felt reassuringly firm and permanent the closer she came to the church.

It was not, of course, that she absolutely needed the reassurance. Now that the long wait was over, the act passed, Rachel felt increasingly calm and passive, cut off from the constant movement of people and things around her. The town, all the folks she knew so well, seemed far away, no longer as intimate and real as they had once been. And Rachel welcomed this peace, this deep, personal stillness and silence within the bustle of things, with its benign presence and sense of conclusion, of things over and done with. She had felt this way most of the day, and the same feeling increased as she walked along. She was almost glad that Peter was not with her.

She was empty, emptied of all passion. Neither fear nor joy, hope nor despair, belief nor doubt were hers. Now, she wanted only to be lost within the crowd of people who would be in the church, to hear Marcus Hawkins repeat with sanguine expectation from the pulpit those memories that she had long ago fixed within her heart. For Peter, belief was not desirable but necessary. For her, belief had always been inevitable. Rachel had known this, too, from the first day of their marriage: how Peter was always searching for proof, a recognition of love when only love was there, real because someone wished it to be, valuable because someone placed value in it. This was Peter's burden, to strive to discover those truths closest to him. Here, here and now, Rachel could strive no more but could finally accept that peace that neither pride nor humility could bring.

It was the end of a long voyage. The bells tolled the final hours in sharp, heavy bursts. But two months ago Thomas had been alive. Thomas and Matthew and James and Isaac, all alive. It was so long ago. The time had been so very hard, Peter wandering around the house from room to room, his distraction and growing desperation only faintly veiled by his pretense of working at his desk or out back, sometimes straightening and rearranging the rooms endlessly one by one.

("See here, Rachel, doesn't the chair look better by the window to catch the morning light? And many a summer's night you'll appreciate the breeze off the Point the window will afford.")

She had made him leave the house, forced him out and to work as she herself worked (and to watch the boys die in such an inconceivable way, one after the other, one by one, each of the same terrible disease, as if some great pestilence had been visited upon them and them alone, as if the children were an atonement for some even greater malefaction, some outrage of which they were unaware but nonetheless culpable and censurable).

The sand was soft and gritty beneath Rachel's shoes, dry in only one day, and it yielded and slipped under her. She felt the steady pressure of Gabriel's forearm hold her up as they came close to the church steps, to walk now this way for the last time the worn, wooden steps, uneven and faded, their yearly coat of paint barely visible at the ends of each board beyond the smooth, whitened handrail. With one hand, Rachel lifted her skirts and mounted the steps into the church. Even the ship's survivors were there, she noted. She was still strangely unable to feel awkward about Peter's absence. She wanted to sleep, to feel her father's big, warm arms about her, to close her eyes and hear him laugh once again as he used to. She failed to notice the staring eyes as she walked up the aisle and sat down in her pew, hers and Peter's and the Wahabs' before them for three... four generations. There was a rustle while Gabriel and Abigail sat down beside her. She began to pray.

To the right of the pulpit Marcus Hawkins prepared himself carefully. Isaac's coffin was placed at the head of the center aisle. It was closed and adorned with what few colorful shrubs and flowers could be found at that time of the year. There were some sea oats to either side, and upon the plain oak casket itself, a small sprig of holly, beach holly, which someone had gathered and placed there, its red berries conspicuous and manifest before the congregation.

Someone coughed. Marcus looked abstractedly toward the back of the church. There was a general stirring of people in their seats. The upright piano began, its sounds tinny and small beneath the high ceiling of the sanctuary. Rachel looked up from her prayer and leaned back against the pew. Marcus smoothed his white collar in preparation for announcing the hymns.

Outside, the sunlight played coldly off the white walls of the church and the surrounding houses, to be consumed by the dry, almost dusty, brown sand. The shore grasses bent easily before the afternoon breeze. Out from shore, a school of dolphins from time to time broke the water's unusually placid surface as they made their way southward down the beach. The village was quiet and still. The flounder that Ed Manners had caught earlier no longer flopped and twitched as they hung alongside the porch, their skins slowly drying in the cool, fitful, afternoon sun. The town was resting, and far off to the south, on the Sound side, the Elizabeth City–Beaufort Ferry sounded its whistle across the wide stretches of empty water.

The service passed quickly. Gabriel Midgett was grateful for that. He was no more grateful, however, than Marcus Hawkins, who, in spite of his position and duties through the years, was unused to tragedy. The events of the last months appalled him. Every year, some few died on the island; but they were blessedly few, and Marcus always made a mental note about how lucky he was not to have to perform many of these onerous tasks. It wasn't that dying was inevitable and, therefore, doubly terrifying. Marcus understood that. He understood, too, that death presented a Christian with the great paradox of his existence, with resurrection and eternal life.

In fact, he could never read the last pages of Luke without shivering a bit in awe of that great act.

> *Ought not Christ to have suffered these*
> *things, and to enter into his glory?*

It was a magnificent passage, fraught with theological implications and poetic imagery, almost too beautiful, too delicately poignant to behold. Christ, the King of Kings, giving Himself as was foretold to this final humiliation, this consummate mystery of God's might and mercy.

Yet none of this knowledge ever seemed satisfactory when Marcus was called to a sickbed, and he secretly dreaded those times with a passion so intense and intimate that he had never even told his wife of his fears. Before a human being in agony, no words were adequate. He was always aware of a kind of sickly unctuousness that his comfort carried with it, a kind of elaborate inappropriateness before this most consummate of acts.

Death was always ugly. That never ceased to shock Marcus Hawkins. What could one say? No matter how much one wanted to help—wanted to give healing words—what could one say of ugliness, of the vulgar putridity of the flesh? It was all too real. The minister was appalled by such human contact, such vulnerability. It always cost him his soul when he was forced to touch a dying person, to hold hands or put his palm upon a sweat-drenched forehead. He did not like to see people lose their dignity so completely, to need others so very much, so unequivocally.

The winter had been bad in this regard. Never had Marcus seen as sickly a season as this one. This fall, malaria had come over from the mainland and visited the islands. It had been an especially hot and fetid September and October. Then, as the winter progressed, everyone had feared a smallpox epidemic after a case was discovered at Manteo, up north. There had been so much general sickness to worry him, and now this. What could he do? Never before had Marcus Hawkins felt so completely used up, so bereft of words. There was little that the service could do, and so Marcus chose to make it short. (Just this side, Gabriel felt, of perfunctory, but hard words and hard doings were needed for hard times.) That Peter did not attend the service only strengthened Marcus in his conviction that this particular tragedy was better forgotten than heeded.

The sermon was short, full of awkward and self-conscious homilies, which seemed painfully transparent to Marcus, although (he kept telling himself) few of the islanders recognized their minister's discomfiture. For them this was death, simply and only death. It was to be expected. Eventually it was to be desired. The Reverend Marcus Hawkins knew that his parishioners felt death explicable, and such knowledge tortured and shamed him. Marcus preached and he suffered. He ended his sermon with a line that repeated itself over and over to him as the congregation sang the final hymn.

> *In him is life; and the life*
> *is the light of men.*

Is and was life. Both had to be so.

The hymn rolled itself against the walls of the church, coating them with a luxurious and resonant piety.

> *This is my Father's world,*
> *And to my listening ears*
> *All nature sings while round me rings*
> *The music of the spheres.*

It was a weak choice, Marcus thought, yet no one minded. He had picked it knowing that no one would. They all liked it in spite of its inappropriateness, its inability to explain all that had happened and might happen again and again before he himself made an end of it.

The pallbearers walked forward to the altar rail and lifted the small, plain casket easily upon their shoulders. Only briefly did Matthew Styron, a young, strapping boy, but a mite clumsy, let his corner fall precariously below the other three. Everyone within the church listened and drew their breaths, but heard nothing. Marcus Hawkins shivered.

The walk to the grave was the hardest part. He had known it would be. Earlier, Marcus had thought to have the service at the Wahab-Howard family cemetery and be done with it, but he had finally dismissed the idea as too unseemly, lacking in decorum for such an important family and singular event.

Outside the church, the bearers placed the casket upon the small, weathered, horse-drawn cart that Tom Aul always kept ready for such occasions and stood back as the wheels began to roll and slip down the road. The congregation had filed out of the church in families, everyone waiting until Rachel, Gabriel, and Abigail made their way to the rear of the cart.

The march was slow and difficult. The family plot was way across town. Marcus wondered again if he had done right. Everyone was tired. The survivors huddled together in the middle of the long line, slipping and puffing through the shifting sand. People talked in low whispers. Occasionally an older boy would detach himself from one group and run ghostlike to another. The younger children were either carried or walked close to their mothers, holding on to the long, voluminous skirts beside them.

The cart creaked as it turned from the church road onto the main street which circled the bay. There were deep ruts in the roadbed, and the horse's splayed hooves dug futilely into the unsubstantial earth. The cart became stuck, and the bearers hurried to push it beyond the intersection. The party, momentarily halted, moved forward. Amens punctuated the stillness of the late afternoon. Marcus sighed. He would have to make the graveside words very short. Rachel seemed too tired for much more of this.

The long line of mourners continued around the bay to the Sound side of the island, turning off the road in front of Mark Terrell's house and moving over the narrow, weed-filled path that led past the Wahab-Howard family plot. Almost every house on Ocracoke had a family cemetery. Few thought it fitting to bury one's kin in a common graveyard. Folks simply went out back and buried their fathers and mothers, their sons and daughters, in simple cross-marked rows, generation upon generation.

The Howard-Wahab plot was only marginally different. It stood across the path from old Bob Howard's house. Four white stone markers outlined its edges. A thick, white rope connected them on three sides and ran thence to a central stone arch, which Job had built facing the road shortly after his father died. Other than this tenuous grandeur and its relatively large size, the cemetery was like all the others on the island. The whitewashed stone markers weathered quickly before the ocean winds and blowing sands. Here and there a stone was wildly askew, the earth beneath it deeply sunken. Small clumps of grass grew in the sand between the tightly packed monuments. At one with its environment, the cemetery was not ugly, but any gentleness or calm and orderly beauty was unknown to it. Three huge live oaks spread themselves upward and in from its corners to cover the graves.

Upon reaching the graveyard, mourners began to queue on each side of the arch. No one but Rachel, Marcus, the bearers, and the Midgetts went into the yard to watch Isaac's plain, undecorated coffin lowered into the open pit. The headstones were too close to permit many people. Marcus stepped carefully as he walked among the severe, sand-torn markers. All were the same slate gray. All were two to three feet high except for the few smaller ones, which denoted children. All had been imported from Morehead City, chiseled and shaped there before shipping by the one stonecutter within a hundred miles of Ocracoke, a man who had seen almost none of the many people whose graves his stones, and those of his father, now marked.

Paint was peeling from the arch, Marcus noted. Muted late afternoon sunlight played around the trees and shadowed the front of the cemetery within a harsh, cold silhouette. Isaac's grave was alongside those of his three brothers. There were three freshly filled mounds beside one another, hardly weeks old. Only the earth over James showed any signs of compacting and blending into the seared and moss-grown patina of the rest of the cemetery. Only James's grave also had a marker. None had yet arrived for the other two. Marcus stood at the head of the pit, and another chill passed along his back and arms. It was cold, a dreadfully clear and cold winter's afternoon. Rachel stood alone, a step or two in front of Gabriel and Abigail, her head bent as if peering down into the blackness of the hole.

Gulls circled and called out to one another across the long reaches of the Sound. How lonely it was. No one was really out there. The little community stood between sea and sea, solitary, shivering in the cold, and burying its dead. Nowhere, far out over the ocean, over the long waters of the Sound, over the vast stretches of dreary, silent marshland, nowhere was there anyone else who knew what was happening.

Even Marcus's own decision to live here, made carefully so long ago in his youth, now seemed alien and unexplainable. What atonement? The flesh constantly escaped him. It was so mutable, so evanescent. What was the sin? Rachel was crying. It was ugly to see her try to hold back her tears, her face distorted, her nose running, and a deep convulsive dry retching shaking her body as Gabriel held her securely in his arm.

When will she stop, he thought. Lord, give her dignity. Where's Peter? Where's Peter at this hour?

Marcus heard himself saying words, but they too were far away, faint and hollow within the evening. "Frail children we are, feeble and frail within God's mighty world...." The gulls squawked louder overhead.

Toward the back of the assembled villagers he saw movement, black and ominous. It was only a heavy, darker shadow under the trees across the road, flickering from tree to tree, its movements tentative and nervous as he finished his short eulogy. "And in the words of the song we shall sing, only 'under the shadow of thy throne shall thy saints dwell secure.'"

There was a dull thud as the coffin struck the earth, then harsh whirring noises as the ropes were pulled out from under it. The burial was taking place right there, thought Marcus. These people would not wait for hours after the mourners had left to retrieve the ropes and fill in the grave.

Marcus looked again across the road and realized that Ezekiel, the Midgetts' old nigger, was back again. Unwilling to join the other mourners, kithless, he hovered about the edges of the crowd.

The song continued, and the minister was glad for its garment of notes, the living cerements which would wrap and enfold the all-too-ugly flesh.

> *O God, our help in ages past,*
> *Our hope for years to come.*

Orderly and precise, how good it was. One could predict its stately, even majestic measures.

> *Our shelter from the stormy blast*
> *And our eternal home.*

For long minutes Marcus stood mouthing the rich phrases of the hymn and staring blankly at the shadow across the road.

*Short as the watch that ends the night
Before the rising sun.*

No one who watched Marcus thought to look back. Those who noticed the rigid preacher's stare merely told themselves that the Reverend Hawkins always was a fine man to conduct a funeral, so sensitive and pious, so sympathetic to the hurt of others.

Before the hymn's end, Ezekiel became nervous when he saw that the minister was staring at him. He hid himself deeper beneath the trees and stole away from the gathering before the others could see him, too. Marcus, the last to leave the graveside, stood still, gazing into the empty woods.

Only Matthew Styron's hand upon his shoulder woke the minister from his dream. He then walked out of the yard and slowly passed Rachel Wahab, touching her hand as he did, assuring her that he would visit on the morrow. In doing so he interrupted young Beatrice O'Neal (quite rudely, he thought afterward, although she had not seemed to mind). Offering his apologies, Marcus continued calmly away toward home.

"Oh, Mrs. Wahab," Beatrice resumed, "I'm so sorry for you. Is there anything that Ma and me can do to help? A body's just never prepared for this. Like when Granpa went away. I was too young to know at the time, but Ma says it was just awful. I only felt kinda squeamish and scared, like there was something terrible and great happenin' that I didn't know."

Rachel clasped the young girl's hand. "Thank you for thinking of us, Beatrice." She was not crying now, and she knew she would cry no more. Gabriel looked around the thinning crowd for Mrs. O'Neal to come and take her daughter.

"Oh, Mrs. Wahab, I'm so sorry. It'll all be fine later on,

won't it? God don't do such things without a reason, you'll see. I know He loves us all, and He's only taken Isaac to his bosom like He'll take us all one day. Oh, Mrs. Wahab, I love you so much and I'm so sorry."

The girl wept. Rachel closed her eyes and held the young, soft body close until Beatrice's mother came and led her away, speaking in low, admonitory tones. Rachel and Gabriel and Abigail walked home in a silence that not one of them dared violate. The house was empty when they arrived. Both Gabriel and Abigail wanted to stay with her, but Rachel would not have it.

"Now it is time to be alone," she said. "You've been so very good to Peter and me, but now we must all be alone awhile."

Against this there was no arguing. Even Gabriel's insistence that he would go and look for Peter rang false. Peter would come home when he was ready. If she needed any help, Rachel could get the Auls soon enough. The husband and wife left. Abigail huddled under Gabriel's arm as he unlatched the front gate and guided her down the path. They walked away swiftly in the stiffening evening breeze. Rachel watched them until they disappeared beyond the lane.

Some time later she turned from the window and went into the kitchen to prepare a warm soup for Peter upon his arrival home. He would be cold and tired from the night air. And she was right. When Peter entered the house, he took off his coat, kissed her, and sat silently at the table with her as they ate.

He did not tell her that he took a long, aimless walk, or that he originally and perversely went out to meet the funeral procession, but arrived late just as Marcus was praying over Isaac's grave. He did not tell his wife that he had been unable to walk further down the path and so stood transfixed, staring at the scene before him until a sharp movement in the woods caught his eye. It was Ezekiel. And, as if moving through a faded picture, Peter had left the path and followed the old man across town to the north road, through the thin tangle of bramble and brush that marked winter upon the island. Then he followed Ezekiel all the way up the Sound side to the small, tidal creek that bisected the island. The old Negro was surprised when Peter came upon him in what looked like a secret retreat of some kind. There were paints and cans, fishing lines, an empty canteen, and amidst the assorted collection that Ezekiel had around him, a strange and singular painting, which fascinated Peter. This had obviously pleased Ezekiel, and he had laughed and rubbed the tough, white whiskers on his dirty face. He and Peter had talked far into the night after that. Ezekiel had even lit a fire in a blackened hole he had dug into the sand (what must have been) years before.

And of all this Peter told Rachel his wife nothing. They ate in silence and unspoken communion, washed and dried the dishes, and then went upstairs to bed. Peter lay that night with his wife in his arms staring up at the gloom of the ceiling, the softness of Rachel's breast pressing against his side and stomach with each breath, until finally his eyes would stay open no longer and he slept.

# XIII

# WANDERER

THE NEXT MORNING was bright and crisp, the wind eddying from the northwest. The cold sun shimmered through the parlor window and warmed the soft green of the walls and couch. It filtered through the curtains and washed deeply into every corner of the hall and sitting room. Peter, down from the bedroom and just awake, blinked his eyes and retreated to the kitchen.

He wanted to visit Ezekiel again; that was why he had risen early. Instead, he lingered in the house, with Rachel asleep upstairs. He feared to leave the house or to leave her in it alone. Unlike himself, Peter decided to fix breakfast before Rachel awoke. She slept late and he was reluctant to wake her. He went about the business of the kitchen with his usual efficiency. It was his habit to share chores with his wife during the long winter months of forced idleness, and now the repeated motions seemed soothing and blessedly simple to him. He stoked the big fireplace in the kitchen and began a small fire in the bedroom to take the chill away when Rachel was about. He went back down to the kitchen and heated a large pot of coffee, set the table, and took out half a loaf of thick, heavy, home-baked bread which they had not eaten at dinner two nights before. He put some honey on the table and milk for Rachel's cereal. There were eggs and bacon in the house if she wanted any, but Peter suspected not, and so he sat down with his own coffee to wait for his wife.

The house was empty and quiet. It turned eight and Rachel was still asleep. Peter went back into the parlor and sat down with his coffee. The painful brightness of the low, early morning sun was gone, and the orderly room pleased him. Even now, shadow and substance were beginning to reappear along the far wall. He sat for a long time in the big overstuffed chair his father had always loved, a gift from Job, and it was fully a half hour before Rachel summoned him out of a sound sleep.

"You were snoring, Peter. At nine in the morning you were snoring." She attempted a smile.

"'Tis not yet nine," he said, embarrassed, rubbing his eyes and looking at the clock. "I've been up since afore six."

"I know. I listened for a while upstairs. You do make such

a racket when you keep house, Peter Wahab. A body would have to be made of stone to sleep through it."

"You've been awake since then?"

"Yes."

"Why didn't you come down? I've had breakfast waiting for you."

"I wanted to be alone a spell, that's all."

"Don't know as I'll ever understand you."

"Mercy, you really did put yourself out, didn't you?" Rachel had moved to the kitchen door, and she clasped her hands in a parody of surprise. "How fine of you, Peter, how really very fine of you."

He became embarrassed again and was aware of his awkwardness. "It's good enough for a late breakfast. If you want dinner, there are eggs and bacon aplenty to be had."

Peter groaned obviously as he rose from the chair; then he stretched himself before entering the kitchen with his wife. He forgot his coffee mug, and Rachel was lucky to refill it with what coffee had not steamed away while he was asleep. Peter sat at the table and watched her move around the room. Swiftly, he thought, swiftly in light but serious womanlike ways. The house was so empty, and yet she still busied herself. Her dress and apron were newly pressed, and she was freshly washed too. He could smell the strong soap odor. His hand brushed over the rough paint of the hard oak table. It was newly scrubbed and cleaned. The floor was newly washed as well. How long Rachel had worked the night before! How could she possibly have done so after the funeral?

Rachel sat down and handed her husband a hot piece of toast. Peter could not talk further, and Rachel suspected that it was not desirable. She watched him and pursed the corners of her lips as he reached across the table for the honey, but she said nothing. The two continued to eat without conversation.

He's thinking about leaving, she said to herself. He's thinking about leaving this place now that all the children are gone, the family all buried or gone who knows where. He doesn't know if he wants to stay any more, to live with me on this island and bide the wind and the sea. The silence hurt her, and it fell like a veil between them, a veil that thoughts alone could not rend. Rachel spoke only to herself.

"Oh, Peter, you're a blessedly simple man. I can see you so clearly. You've never liked it here, have you, with Job always giving you those wild ideas, never letting your heart rest a little? Why can't you give it all up? You're sitting, wanting to leave, aren't you? But where would we go, Peter, where? I'd not let you leave alone, not after all these restless years. Certainly not up north. It's two hundred miles 'cross sound and swamp to Raleigh, and then what would you do? No, husband, you'll stay here awhile, no matter what you might think. You're an islander. Lord, we all are, and no teachin' or learnin' will wash away what this living writes upon our souls. There's no place to go, Peter. I've known it for years. This is home no matter . . . ."

Peter pushed his chair back from the table. Rachel was surprised at how easily she had forgotten his physical presence. The steam from her coffee was barely perceptible. There was a seam tearing in Peter's overalls. They would need tending to after supper.

"Well, I'll be about my chores now."

"So soon, Peter? Why not sit a bit? They'll all wait your time."

"No. My time's now. The nets still need mending. I've not been about it for some time, and such can't wait all winter."

"Shall I wait dinner for you? We can eat late if you want."

Peter Wahab paused. Dinner was a normal thing, a matter of course. Why did his wife ask if it was to be ready? Did she know that he still had a mind to see Ezekiel, that he couldn't forget the strange, haunting presences that slumbered within the folds of those dark clouds?

No. She couldn't read his thoughts, not even after all these years. Of course, yesterday had been an end of it. All meals would be different now. How he wished to leave all this behind, but there was no place to go. He played with the hitch on his overall straps and adjusted it absentmindedly before he spoke again.

"Yes, I'll . . . . No, no don't wait on me, I'll keep myself until tonight. . . . I've got some errands to accomplish around the village. I want to thank Tom and Gabriel and Elizabeth. I might just walk over to the store as well. We'll have an early supper."

Peter turned in the doorway and looked back into the shadowed kitchen. "I'll be in the shed for an hour or two. When it gets near dinner, you might give me a call. If I'm still around, I'll come and sit a spell with you, but don't you fix me anything. It's too late in the day as it is, and I've a mind to take a walk up the shore later on."

Through the rest of the morning, Peter worked on his nets. Across the yard, every so often he'd hear Rachel moving about the house, but the day was unusually calm and peaceful, not even broken by the sound of visitors. He was thankful that the nets had remained dry during the storm and that he did not have to go out into the yard to lay and string them. True, it was awkward, certainly more difficult, to see and to mend the weak and shredded strand of rope inside the shed, but he did not want to stand shivering in the cold, bright light of the midday sun either. The sheen off the bare yard would be too blinding to allow him to work comfortably.

Noon came and passed while he worked patiently on the nets. Rachel did not call him. Once or twice he looked cautiously toward the house, then squinted at his work. It was not good work; Peter knew he could do much better, but the cramped space and dim light wouldn't allow it. Besides, he tired more quickly the older he got. It was noticeable these last years.

About two o'clock, Peter folded the nets as best he could and walked out the side gate onto the road toward Tom Aul's house. Shadows from the pines and oak were starting to fall across the path, and he walked faster than usual without realizing it. The stops at Tom Aul's and Gabriel's were courtesy. Peter relied upon their shortness but was still relieved when neither man attempted much talk. He also tried not to show his impatience when talking with Elizabeth Turner, but felt a little embarrassed when finally he told her that Rachel was fixing an early supper and he was, therefore, a mite pressed for time. Elizabeth laughed, then blushed before apologizing.

"I just talk myself sick sometimes, Peter, I really do. Now you go tell Rachel I'll see her tomorrow and we'll talk woman-talk without you."

She released him. At almost a trot, he set out for the creek where he'd seen Ezekiel the night before. Nothing explicitly told him that the old Negro would be there, hidden by the lush patchwork of vegetation along the creek's banks. Nothing told him that the painting, subtle and disturbingly evocative, as if death itself were an unending satisfaction of forbidden pleasures, would be there. But Peter felt it, as if a premonition had come to him after these many years, and he was to begin, not end, a long, long journey into his own soul.

When he arrived at the creek, he was breathing heavily after the long walk through the remains of grass, which had grown waist high during the summer and then blanketed the sand with a thick refuse of vegetation by midwinter. He peered anxiously into the little copse. Protected by the canopying bushes and shrubs, it was dark within, and he could not make out Ezekiel's presence.

"Ezekiel . . . Ezekiel . . . you there?"

Ezekiel looked around, startled. He had been gazing sleepily at his painting and had not heard Peter's approaching steps. He wasn't afraid. He'd pretty much suspected that Peter would be back after the night before, but when it had gotten on towards noon and then one or two, he'd left off waiting. Needn't worry about it much, he'd told himself. Mr. Peter would be back one day.

"Yes, sir. I's here, Mr. Peter. Right here."

Peter bent down and crawled into the little copse, grimacing as he smelled the Negro's raw, stale odor. He couldn't remember being so close to Ezekiel before in such a confined place. Yet . . . last night. Did the old Negro smell like this last night, too? He realized that he himself was sweating.

'You been here all day, Ezekiel?" Peter asked as he seated himself tentatively next to the Negro and looked past him toward the painting only a few feet away, half within the copse and half within the brilliant sheen of a late afternoon sun. He rubbed his eyes and felt his own clean-shaven face as Ezekiel's hand picked at the wiry, white bristles along his cheek. "It's a long time to stay here, Ezekiel. Aren't you hungry? It doesn't look as though you left this place all night."

The Negro laughed. "Oh, I been gone, Mr. Peter." Ezekiel was now looking at the painting as well, his right hand playing with the unshaven hair on his throat. "Been down to Mr. Gabriel's house early this mornin'. I been doin' all right." Ezekiel chuckled and rocked back and forth on his heels and buttocks as he sat against the slightly rising bank of the stream.

Strange, thought Peter, this must be the first time he's ever not risen to greet me. Course, you can't do it here, but he never even tried.

"Zeke . . . ."

"Yes, yes sir." Ezekiel was chuckling and rocking harder, looking beyond the copse over the sunlit dunes to the east. "Ole Zekiel, he get along all right, all right. Ain't no moss on his shoes, no sir, no sir. Why—ole Zekiel even ketched his own supper today, ha-ha, ketched it with a string and a sinker, he did. They all says it can't be done, but ole Zekiel did it. He ketched those ole flat fish for dinner just as quick as that."

The Negro interrupted his rocking motion long enough to snap his fingers, then smiled and continued on. "They're your dinner, too, if you want, Mr. Peter. 'Cause I knew you'd be back." Ezekiel laughed again, too proud to contain himself. "Be back to see that, huh?" He pointed to the painting with one hand, holding his knees with the other and continuing to rock more slowly now. "Back to see the ole nigger's paintin', huh? They never looked much at my paintin's before, but this one they gotta see. Can't help it. Gotta look at this paintin'—whether you wants to or not. Yes sir, that's some paintin'. Some paintin'."

Peter shifted his weight laboriously and brushed Ezekiel's shoulder. The Negro never noticed. Peter was growing impatient with the grizzled old man. What did he care about flounder and lines and sinkers? Everyone knew that Ezekiel could catch fish when other men could not even find them. The Negro's all-too-evident and childish pride annoyed him. This was not a time for laughter, and Peter could not help feeling that the old man's joy was insensitive and ill mannered. He wanted this other person to serve him and his needs. He envied the old man's self-satisfaction at the painting's creation, and he wanted him to be more humble, more reticent before his own loss.

"Well—get on with it, Ezekiel. Get on with it. Tell me what the painting's about."

Ezekiel stopped rocking abruptly and looked at Peter. The Negro's unabashed stare and surprise made Peter all the more uncomfortable. He tried to ignore the silence by looking at the painting, but he couldn't.

"Well, Ezekiel! What you staring at so?" He heard himself fall into the colloquial and was annoyed.

"But—but you already know, Mr. Peter. I told you last night all about it. All about it, don't you remember? The clouds and the storm, fiercest there ever was on this island. The skies was angry, angry as God's wrath upon the children of Israel. They'd come all the way across an ocean here, an' I tole those people, I tole 'em."

"I know, I know, Ezekiel." It was an old story. Everyone remembered how Ezekiel had warned the Ocracokers of the great hurricane so many years back. Every time Ezekiel told it, the story grew more and more fantastic. Now the hurricane was a compilation of all the island's storms. To listen to the Negro, one would think that every inlet along the coast had been cut by that one, fierce storm.

"Oh, you don't know, Mr. Peter. No, you don't know."

The old Negro would never have taken such liberties with another white man, Peter thought. It was because of their long years of friendship. And yet, Gabriel, too, had always been kind to him.

Ezekiel seemed distracted. When was it the Negro began to lose his senses? He'd always been a little queer, ever since he was a little boy trailin' after his mamma's skirts. But it had gotten worse as the years went along. Ezekiel had never been like other men, much less other niggers.

"And it cut Ocracoke inlet right through, it did. I watched those clouds. Lord, they run up to God's heaven and hollered down at us 'cross great holes in the sky. Oh, it was a fearful night, a fearsome thing to see. Fearsome it was."

"And justice, too, Ezekiel." Peter felt compelled to say it. "High judgment and might was in that hurricane. But you talked about more last night, don't you remember? You spoke of Deborah and your mamma. You said they were in the picture. And I said that Job knew your mamma, but you wouldn't say no more, and I had to leave you."

Ezekiel seemed not to understand and stared at him

blankly. "Deborah? Deborah—oh, she my granmamma. She came from far away. Ole Pharaoh never knew her. She came from far away, but not from Egypt land. No, no, not Deborah."

Peter was in anguish. The old Negro refused to listen, refused to understand him. "No, not Deborah, Ezekiel. I know who she was, your granmamma. Deborah came from far away. She was a mainlander, from up north. I mean your mamma who bore you and brought you up. Job knew her. Where's she in your picture?"

"Oh, no, no, Mr. Peter. Deborah was the chile of another king, stole into bondage in the desert, 'cross the seas. And they sing songs to her beyond the mountains still. No, she never was Pharaoh's chile. She live in a strange, dark land you and I never saw and never will."

"Deborah—your mamma, I don't care who, Ezekiel. Are they in the picture—for God's sake, will you listen to me and stop carrying on so?" Peter was clutching the old man firmly by the shoulders, their faces only inches apart within the dim, moist copse. Ezekiel stopped, watched with an artless, incredulous countenance as Peter sat back, and then he crooned softly in a low, cooing voice, which Peter strained to hear.

"Deborah, Deborah. No, Mr. Peter, Deborah's not in there, not in that picture . . . ."

"But, you said . . . ."

"I never said no such thing." Ezekiel was disconcerted by his own temerity. "I mean I don't remember no such thing. I'm just an ole nigger anyhow."

Peter was losing him. He didn't want that. "Well, what did you say, Ezekiel? Tell me what you did say."

Ezekiel hesitated, as if lost for words, then went on. "That they all went out from Egypt land, that they all went out and they was alone and lost." Ezekiel began to chant and his eyelids drooped. "They all went out and Deborah was stolen away, with her sisters, over the great sea, they sailed on for days and days, close together, close as sardines, livin' and dyin' in the bowels of the whale, every one. And they was cast upon a strange place to live out their days, live them out in exile away from their homeland.

"But the Seven Sisters was still together, every one. And they led their people through the world, never cryin' but only remberin' the great kingdom they'd left, but never in their hearts, even when they learned to pray before a new God, a God who at first they couldn't touch but who they came to love more than their masters and He them, too.

"And Deborah was the most beautiful of them all. The storms never changed her. She was like Judith, 'cept she never ran away. Deborah was...."

> *How hath the Lord covered the daughter*
> *of Zion with a cloud in his anger,*
> *and cast down from heaven unto the earth*
> *the beauty of Israel, and remembered not*
> *his footstool in the day of his anger.*

"But why was He angry? Why was He angry, Ezekiel?" Peter wanted him to keep talking.

"Angry?" the old Negro was confused. "Who's angry, Mr. Peter? I'm not angry."

"No, I mean . . . why was Deborah so used, treated so—as she was? It wasn't right!"

"Why—why—that don't make no difference, Mr. Peter. It don't make no difference why you suffer. Deborah watched almost her whole fam'ly die, some on the long sea voyage, others in a foreign land. She never knowed why. They all worked hard in them fields—and at night, at night they sung of their freedom and the good land they left behind. It don't make no difference...."

"Yes it does, Ezekiel. Yes it does. It isn't right that such a thing should happen. It isn't right that Judith should leave us and never return, that a man should be left without kin or home."

Ezekiel thought for a long time. The silence penetrated into the bones of both men. Only the wind whistled constantly and evenly across the island.

"That Judith—she gone, Mr. Peter," Ezekiel finally said as he looked at the painting. "See, she's not even in there like all the rest. She gone for good. Nobody who goes up north ever comes back. You might's well make your mind up. That girl gone for good. Deborah came to the islands to get well, and that girl ran away to get well. Lord only knows what happened to her."

"But that's not right, Ezekiel. God has no right to do that, to take away Job's only child, my . . . ."

"God don't do that, Mr. Peter." Ezekiel ran his hand over the sand-gritted canvas. He stared intently at its surface. "Men do that. Only men run away, Mr. Peter, not God. Judith ran away because *she* want to. She ain't never comin' back."

Peter blinked. What had the old man said? He was unable to see the painting well in this light, but he felt the old man's artless candor. He watched Ezekiel's gnarled hands move over the stick figures at the bottom edges of the painting. They were strewn every which way, absurd and lifeless dolls beneath the storm's fury. But the storm seemed not to care, lost in its own ecstatic motion.

"How do you know that, Ezekiel? How do you know that for sure?" His own voice was hollow and strained. Strangely, he heard himself as if he were another person whose eyes searched far over the tangle of brush and sand toward the horizon but who never moved.

"Know what, Mr. Peter?" The Negro waited briefly for a reply that didn't come and then smiled broadly and proceeded to tell his story. It wasn't often that he had such an audience, and Ezekiel was beginning to enjoy his new-found power. He wanted to tell Mr. Peter everything, all those deep, abiding secrets he had so long denied his own straining soul, which had thus lain inert within him only to find their way onto his canvasses, wild and without structure but not without form, bearing the fruits of his lonely and marginal life—the memories of generations of those who had lived as he did.

"Oh, the Lord God knows all, Mr. Peter, but Judith, she run away. She was a wild one, that girl, no doubt about it. She just like old Deborah, Mr. Peter, just like her. You remember when old Deborah died, how lonely she was? She couldn't go back neither. A lost chile that woman was, a lost chile, cold and lonely here with white folk, but lost to her own kind too. That's why she had to stay here, why she couldn't go back. No, sir, couldn't ever go back."

The old man was talking more to the air than to Peter, and the white man sat amazed and abashed at the intimacy implied by the Negro's reverie. It was a story with huge gaps as Ezekiel unfolded it, and his listener continually strove to understand the moment and significance that even brief and subordinate passages seemed to have for Ezekiel.

The Negro told how Deborah had come from Africa and almost died of sickness on the boat. No island sickness was to kill her later, only heartbreak when she'd look out over the long stretches of ocean. (Every mornin' she'd see the sun rise out of Miz Midgett's kitchen up on Hatteras.) Peter, his own hurt in abeyance before the vast history Ezekiel told, made out that Deborah had been used poorly by one of Nixon's foremen, possibly raped, possibly not. Ezekiel saw the act as both necessary and inevitable, an extravagant joining of the Lord's own mysterious polarities. (Black and white they was, and her grippin' that jewel as tight as death itself.) That was why years later Deborah never went back to the plantation. Pregnant with Ezekiel's mother, she had borne her child upon the island, endured a second exile away from her own people, and finally wandered off, well enough forgotten, down Hatteras to the Cape. She was dead to her people and dead to the Nixons, who thought her perished of disease upon the island. She had endured the last, long years in welcomed seclusion, lost to two worlds and unborn to another.

"That's why she never could come back. No, sir. No more than Judith could. You mustn't wait. She was a queen, Mr. Peter, a lost queen, my mamma told me. Sometimes it happens that way. It just does. Lord, He don't do for men what they do themselves, but He knows it there, and He watchin' all the time. Like when they all didn't listen to me, all those Ocracokers. Lord knew that, but He sent me anyway for my sake, yes sir." Ezekiel gripped his knees and rolled back again on his buttocks. "Sent me for my own sake, only I didn't know it at the time. It took a spell to see it. It took a spell."

"That's quite a story, Ezekiel." Peter felt acutely embarrassed. He didn't know how to treat this old man who had so naively given himself away over the last hour. In a very short time Ezekiel had become a stranger to him. So much had happened to the old man of which he himself had never dreamed. He felt inadequate and out of place here under the live oak, staring at the still, wondrous brilliance of the painting.

"Yes sir, it that all right. Sure is that. Quite a story. No doubt it sure is that, Mr. Peter. No doubt. Why, I'm Deborah's son just as sure as you're Miss Judith's. I sure am."

"I'm what?" Peter was startled by the Negro's remark, more by its casualness than by its literalness. Yet it still took him a moment to realize that he was not Judith's earthly son at all, that she could have no son who would be his brother.

"Why, you're some fine man, Mr. Peter, a fine, kind, and good man. Anybody ask me and I'll tell 'em. You're a fine man. But you're like Judith, too. Like my mamma tole me about her. You're proud, proud and strong, just like she was, and Deborah, too."

Peter winced and pulled himself to his knees. It was time to go. The old man was starting to carry on again and the hour was too late for that. Who in hell was this man, anyway, to lecture him any longer with stories that couldn't end and legends mixed with lies?

"Like the old tree. You're proud like that old tree, Mr. Peter." Ezekiel was proud of his imagination, his resourcefulness. "Pharaoh knew. He knew. That old mud dobber."

(An old, solitary wasp, waiting alone for its own death, a dirt dauber building its own sarcophagus out of the cracked earth around it. Ezekiel was a mud dauber. The villagers often called him so in fun. Yet how apt the name was for Job, a scarred and lonely wasp waiting to die.)

"What did Job know, Ezekiel? What in the Lord are you talkin' about anyway?" Peter stood up and brushed the sand from his trousers.

"That ole tree, Mr. Peter. I'm talkin' about that ole tree. Pharaoh knew. He knew it couldn't live up here. Too cold, too fierce for it. But he brought it anyway, and it lived. It did live."

"Is that what you call living, Ezekiel? Why you old fool, the tree's half-dead in the summer and worse every winter. Look at it now. That tree's dying, not living. You don't know what you're talking about, Ezekiel. That tree's not free to live. It's in chains and Job should never have brought it here."

"Ain't none of us free, Mr. Peter. None of us. Even that ole mud dobber, he's not free. Pharaoh, he wanted a friend. That's why he brought that tree. Miss Judith, she wanted a friend, and that's why she left."

Ezekiel slouched uneasily against the live oak's twisted trunk. With the white man standing, he did not feel at ease to sit any longer, yet standing was clearly awkward for him in the confined space beside the stream.

"Ain't no freedom in bein' all alone and prideful, no sirree."

"Sit down, old man. I'm leaving." Peter's voice was peremptory. It cracked through the cold, evening air. "I've had enough of this talk. There's a world a difference between Job and Judith. That woman was willful and proud. Job was a humble man all his life. He should have been better paid for that than he was, than his father before him was; but it didn't happen, and only God knows why."

"Yes sir, Mr. Peter, God only knows. And we never will. No sir. We never will and we mustn't ask." Ezekiel cowered in the darkness.

Astonished, Peter turned to leave, but a strand of spider web from the overhanging branches fell across his face, momentarily binding him to the spot. He stumbled back, blew up over his face, and brushed the web away. Then he turned to Ezekiel.

"I was a damned fool to come here, old man, a damned fool. You carry on just like everybody says you do, about a world you've never seen and a land you've never been to. I don't understand it and I doubt if you do. And that picture." Peter pointed toward the painting, black and undecipherable under the evening shadows. "That picture of yours ain't finished neither. Look at it, where it's all smudged and gray. You got a lot to do yet, Ezekiel, a whole lot."

"Yes sir, yes I do, that ain't no lie." Ezekiel quailed against the tree. "I got a whole lot to do. You're right as rain, I got a whole lot to do."

But as he walked back down the island's length, Peter lost his certainty. There was little left to do on the painting, and he could not believe himself a fool for listening to the Negro's story. The sand slipped beneath his boots as he gained the bare pathway near town's edge and hurried along it.

"Another storm's brewin', Mr. Peter," Ezekiel had called as he left, "so you take care now. These cold nights ain't fit for man or beast to be out."

Another storm. It was a black night and not a cloud all day. How did the old man know there would be another storm? Yet, Ezekiel had been by the shore all day, and he did not doubt that the dirty, tick-bitten Negro was right. Peter gathered the collar of his coat around him as he saw the lights of the cottage. Rachel was up, waiting, and there would be hot food for him in the kitchen.

# XIV

# DIALOGUE

WEDNESDAY, Peter again woke early and dressed alone. The silence of the cottage hovered about him, and he wanted to get an early start to check the horses at the far end of the island, work that he had neglected for three full days since the storm. What was more, Rachel had not reminded him of it, and that was unlike her. Normally she would have offered to help with the stock, for she was as fine a horsewoman as any on the island. Rachel was always there. She always saw to what he forgot, and yet he rarely acknowledged that to her—or to anyone else for that matter. Peter wondered if he had been so very distant during the last two months. How could he have forgotten something as important as seeing to the stock in winter, and why would Rachel not have reminded him? He accused himself this way, and for the first time in days he felt in control of himself. He would see to the ponies; that he could do if little else.

Rachel stirred in the bed, and he moved across the room to the old, ridiculously overstuffed, blue armchair of his father's. Ugly, but his mother had always loved it. When he finished lacing his boots, Peter moved quietly to the desk and left a short note for Rachel saying that he would be home before the evening meal and that she should expect him. These last days had been terribly hard upon her. She had to be very, very tired. He went downstairs, put coffee over the banked coals, and fixed himself a lunch. After breakfast he went to the barn, saddled the only pony kept upon the property, and rode out into the still, dark night.

When Peter arrived at Ocracoke's northern tip, the cold, biting wind of a gray dawn had fully awakened him. Across the inlet, he could barely see the light and smoke of Hatteras. There were less than five hundred people in the town, and yet even that was a great multitude beside the two hundred souls upon Ocracoke. How close the larger village seemed, yet how far away across that expanse of water, which took hours to cross in a bad sea such as was brewing.

Peter knew that the survivors had not left the island, and this storm would keep them at least another three days till the mail boat could make its weekend run.

The wind blew salt spray in his face, and Peter backed his

pony nearer to the dunes. The day's work would be hard and tedious. The ponies upon the island roamed wild throughout the year, carrying only the brand of their owners.

They weren't even ponies, although everyone called them so. They were horses: small, but larger than Shetlands, descended from a shipload of Arabian horses that had wrecked upon the island centuries before. Those animals had given rise to small, sturdy, increasingly thick-coated offspring which lived amazingly well off the sparse vegetation of the island. Over the years, Ocracokers had divided the herd and come to use it largely as a source of money through the sale of older ponies and yearlings. Once a year, there was a general penning, branding, and sale of the ponies, but otherwise they were left alone, hardly cared for at all.

Peter planned to work his way south toward the village. The thick coats of the healthier horses would protect them during the storm, and Peter didn't intend to herd all of the over two hundred ponies to his own pen. To do that would have required six or seven men to span the island's width. Rather, Peter was looking for sick and hurt animals or for late-born foals. If he found any, he was going to drive these toward the Sound side of the island, care for those he could, see the horses into generally protected areas before the rain and wind broke, and take any others back to the barn if need be. The work was arduous and long.

Peter kept crisscrossing the island all morning. At ten o'clock he found one foal newly born just beside a thick growth of yaupon and cedar near the Sound side, three miles or so down the beach. At first he mentally noted that he would have to come back and take the colt home with him later in the day, but after dismounting and checking the animal, he decided that it was at least three days old, possibly born right in the teeth of the previous storm, and it seemed in excellent health. Peter decided to leave it with its mare instead. As the hours passed, he found himself driving two old mares and a yearling colt steadily southward. All seemed in need of care, both mares limping distinctly and the colt with an ugly gash across its back and withers which was infected and needed cleaning. The wind had risen all morning, and as Peter stopped for lunch, it blew steadily from the northeast, whipping great whitecaps upon the sea.

The sea, it was eternal, not this land and forest he had always thought so. All was at the command of the wind and waves. How harshly beautiful it was, the water leaping in rapturous agony far out beyond the beach. He looked northeast toward the cutting edge of the wind and thought he could see the white ocean over the angry tip of Diamond Shoals. He wanted pain. And as much as he had previously avoided it, he now sought it out—avidly, eagerly, as if he were some bewildered lover tormented by his own impassioned dreams. The waves rose to high, angry caps only moments before sinking into deep, huge troughs, and then they rose again to break upon the beach in a constant roar. It was exciting to watch, to feel the wind and sand burning at his face. And this ancient drama, cold and faceless in its seeming dissolution, endured and persisted regardless of him. He could neither change it nor approve of it, terrible in its unconcern and magnificent in its permanence.

Peter started to gather sticks and kindling for a small fire and moved behind a large dune to have his meal out of the wind. Within a few minutes, he built a small fire close under the dune's leeward base and began heating coffee. After the bitter morning's work, the warm, pungent odor made his mouth water, and he took off his pony the cold sandwiches and tin cup he had packed for himself earlier.

"Good day to you, Peter Wahab. Might I join you awhile?" Gabriel Midgett's voice was thin and astringent against the wind. He had ridden in from the south unnoticed, and now dismounted with an exaggerated gesture of friendliness and weariness. Surprised, Peter greeted the big man but did not move from where he stood.

"You're a long way from the station, Gabriel, and it's a mighty raw day."

Gabriel seemed not to notice the unstated question but answered it anyway as he led his pony under the dune next to Peter's.

"Nothin' much about that the boys can't handle. You look in need of some help out here. We can't let you do all our work for us. Is that coffee you've got there?" Gabriel warmed his hands over the fire, rubbing them briskly together; then he took a cup from his knapsack and sat down with a groan. Peter filled it along with his own, and the two men sat for a few minutes before continuing the afternoon's work.

Gabriel broke the silence almost casually. "You have a fight with Rachel this mornin', Peter?"

Peter thought that Gabriel Midgett was usually more tactful. He tried to hide his smile. "What's that, Gabriel? Why, where'd you come by such a notion?"

"I know it ain't none of my business, Peter." Gabriel continued slowly without looking at his friend. "Now I know that very well, but—these last days have been hard for you, for the both of you, and you should know that, and—well, I was over to your place this mornin' after breakfast, and I could tell Rachel was feelin' poorly. Peter, I got to be honest about this. The woman needs your help. You can't go on silent and alone, not comin' home till after dark, leavin' before sunrise. Good God, man, you're alive. No amount of grievin' and guilt is goin' to change that. You've got to give that woman some help. She can't go on like this much longer."

Peter drank his coffee slowly and brushed some sand from his overalls. He threw a sandwich across the fire to Gabriel and began to eat.

Lord, was Gabriel right? Had he been ignoring Rachel so? Why, of course. Even the note must have seemed only an excuse.

"What have I done, Gabriel?" Why should he defer to Gabriel? The big man seemed to feel none of his own awkwardness. Like the sea, thought Peter, disinterested like the sea.

"You've left your wife alone, Peter, that's what you've done, left her alone during those days in which the boys died, left her alone Sunday last, left her so at the cemetery, and now each day you leave her, and all of us, to wander out here doing God knows what—or that which each of us has been doing for you already."

"But the stock must be tended."

"Lord, man, we've been doin' that for days. We all have some ponies out here. Do you think takin' those two lame mares back to the barn will help them any? The gray's old and dyin', Peter. Leave her be. The brown's already been tended to by Ed Manners yesterday morn. Will you not let us help you, Peter? Must you forever search for ways to suffer through this time alone? It isn't so, you know. There've been three deaths besides your boys these last three months. It's been a terrible time for us all, old and young alike. 'Tis no easy time we have of it here, nor never was."

Gabriel drank his coffee and looked away. It was hurting him to say these things.

Peter saw his friend's knuckles whitened around the still-steaming coffee. But what could he say? He had not meant to do all these things, and yet the implications of his actions were undeniably as Gabriel had described them. Had he really meant to hurt all these people, and possibly himself as well? The brief silence now unnerved Peter even more. He wanted to talk. A gust of wind blew sand across his cheek. He looked toward the Sound and squinted his eyes. Even the birds were

*old, thou shalt stretch forth thy hands,
and another shall gird thee, and carry thee
whither thou wouldest not.*

"Peter, listen. Don't ask impossible questions. Be practical. Live here with the rest of us. This visitation cannot be changed. I've lived with you long enough, Peter. You must not bargain with God any more. You dare not be alone any longer. What is in store for us will be, and what remains we must take comfort from. You must go home."

Peter looked out across the dunes. "It's another storm, Gabriel, that will tear up the beach—"

"And that's another thing. Bless it, man, you mustn't live with these pictures always eatin' at you. The beach will be here tomorrow. Change as it may, you won't outlive it. Does it really matter where this island may be next year? We're not the sand but only a speck upon it. God's in the people around you, Peter, in what you do every day. There's no illumination the likes of which you speak of. Love your friends and neighbors, and do for them as you would do for your own.

"I remember once you and I were fishin' on the beach years ago. The weather was good, the sea a bit high, the tide runnin' in, and the sunlight skitterin' over the mornin' dunes like glass. It was a good day for fishin' too, and we were pullin' in sea bass and blue just as fast as you could get a line out. The day, all blue and clear with spring but a smell or two away.

"There was even a school of bottlenose jumpin' offshore, workin' their way down the beach. I turned to point them out and saw you holdin' an empty line in your hand, your face as blank as could be just lookin' down at the sand. I don't know ever what got into you 'cause I called you twice and you didn't listen, just stood there starin'. When I finally shook you by the arm, it took you almost a minute to remember where you were and answer me. You were always like that, Peter, always floatin' off somewhere by yourself, scuddin' before the wind."

The big man smiled, brushed his lips dry with the back of his sleeve, and reached for more coffee. "Do you remember that, Peter? Do you remember what you were doin', Peter?"

"No, Gabriel, I don't." Peter stood up and brushed the seat of his trousers. "It's gettin' on some. We'd best be movin' down toward the village."

"You were lookin' at a sandpiper, Peter. Not really a sandpiper, even, but a sandpiper's prints in the sand. That's all. Lord, I almost blessed you out that day. Lookin' at the prints of a sandpiper in the sand, so curious that you forgot about me and fishin' and the whole world for that matter. 'Look, Gabriel,' you said to me, 'a sandpiper's prints. He was there just minutes ago, and soon even the prints will be gone.'"

Gabriel shook his head. "God bless me, Peter, I'll never understand it. Don't think, Peter, feel. It's surer that way and safer. Come on home and let's you and I and Abigail and Rachel sit down to supper."

"Lord, man, don't you think I feel?"

Peter's disbelief as he looked down upon Gabriel surprised his friend and made him ashamed of his own clumsiness.

"How can you say that, Gabriel? And how can a man feel without thinking? I don't understand that either. The bird's prints are gone. Do you see them? I don't know where they are." Peter looked about him, wildly mocking the emptiness.

The two men remained silent for a long time. There seemed nothing more to say, nothing that could alleviate or change their own mute duality. Each was constrained by his own deep and inexplicable knowledge, knowledge that brought with it the equal constraints of ignorance. And this rent, this sharp, terrible void between such old friends, this humbled them and made them silent.

"And Judith?"

"Judith was just a girl, Peter." Gabriel spoke without looking at his friend. "Just a girl, a little good and a little bad like the rest of us, who wanted to get away. That's all there is to it, and she ain't never comin' back."

Peter was silent a long while.

"Well, Gabriel, let us get on with it. There's work to be done before we get home, and surely we must not keep the women waiting overly much for us."

Gabriel said nothing. The two men put out the fire, stowed their gear, and mounted up. The rest of the afternoon was spent in work Gabriel had thought unnecessary. They continued crisscrossing the island, checking the copses and Sound side for hurt or sick animals. Peter hurried the job as fast as he could, but driving the three ponies before them slowed things up considerably. At one point on the open beach, Peter brought his own pony up short and stared in amazement out to sea.

"She's gone." He called to Gabriel, not far away. "The *Home's* gone."

Gabriel rode up and reined his pony next to Peter's. "Yes, she sure is, Peter. Went in the storm Saturday night. Tore the fo'c'sle apart. Some planking washed up further down the beach a mile or two, but that'll probably go in this next one."

"After all these years. It doesn't seem possible. The old *Home* gone and all those people."

"All those people died many years ago, Peter." Gabriel laughed in surprise. "And there'll be other wrecks to scar the beach in years to come."

Peter leaned across his pony's neck and stroked the thick, wooly fur of the animal's mane. "And, I suppose, many other ponies, too. Nags to carry lights from their necks and show safe passage where there is none. Then we'll gather up the rubbish. Lonely as we are, Gabriel, we'll draw them to us. Because the sea is most beautiful when it's like this."

Gabriel grimaced at his friend and turned his pony toward the dunes.

The rest of the work went quickly in the fading hours of sunlight. Gabriel had said there was really little to do that had not already been done. The stock was healthy and well protected from the storm, with most of the animals already bedded down awaiting the long, cold night. The riders passed them by and, pulling their collars close around their necks, rode before the stiffening wind toward the village.

As they came into town, the wind let up a bit, and Peter reined his pony behind a small grove of cedar .

"Was that Ezekiel up the beach?"

"Yes, it was. I saw him, too. Collectin' shells and such, no doubt, like always. He'll be there tomorrow mornin'. Strange —I saw him Sunday night on the beach. He acted almost mad."

"They say he grinds them for his colors."

"They say a lot of darned nonsense, too. He gets most of his colors from me—or Howard up Hatteras way. Even the Styrons have given him some at times. Got a good collection of shells, though, best on the island, I'd say, for what that's worth. Good ones unbroken aren't as plentiful here as farther south."

"I saw him last night."

"I suspected as much."

The two men were at the junction where they had to part.

"The storm will hold off for a few hours yet. You gather Rachel and come over for supper. Abigail's already told her I was on my way to fetch you."

"You knew I'd seen Ezekiel?" Peter couldn't hide his bewilderment. "I was with him most of the day yesterday."

"No, Peter, I didn't know. I just suspected." Gabriel found a comfortable position on his saddle. His pony pawed the sand. "Ezekiel was around town most of today lookin' for you. He had a paintin' he carried with him and wouldn't show it to a soul. Anyone come near him and he'd hide it from sight and move on out of their way. He was actin' real peculiar, and when I found you'd left home early, I decided I'd better get on out to see you."

The men were quiet again as they'd been for so much of the day after they had begun work.

"Don't do it, Peter. Don't believe what that old, crazy nigger has. Whatever it is, it's not for you. He's been doin' that for years. Ain't a house in town without one of those things on the back porch."

"Where'd he go, Gabriel? Do you know?"

Overhead, the clouds swirled summarily upon one another in fleeting conjunction. It was almost dark. The houses had acquired the gray and notched configuration of the sky.

"No, I don't, and don't you go chasin' him, neither. You've got a sight more to do than go lookin' for that old nigger all over the island."

"No, no—I won't do that, Gabriel. I'll get these animals in the barn and be over with Rachel shortly. Thank you, Gabriel, for the help. I'll remember."

The two men parted. Peter urged his mount down the path with the three ponies shambling along in front of him. He had done this many times before, this same act, the ponies in front of him, tired at day's end, the cedar and oak casting shadows almost indistinguishable from the general darkness. He had done it all before, and now, in spite of himself, this act seemed no different. He remembered too that he was good at figures, that old Job had relied upon him during those last years. Peter felt he was free now, but from what he did not know. And the burden had not been lifted suddenly. It had happened slowly, uncertainly, like the final revolution of a wheel that a small boy might spin aimlessly upon an overturned cart.

The sand squirmed beneath the pony's hooves as it entered the open gate of the yard. To the west, the Sound was still calm and in sharp contrast to the ocean he had just left. There were no birds in the sky and even the few night insects were silent. Only the heavens moved in and out behind the blackened clouds.

# XV

# HOME

PETER DISMOUNTED and herded the ponies into the barn. He wanted to finish his work quickly and speak with Rachel, so he rubbed down his own pony only lightly and then left the barn door tied open. If the animals wanted to leave, they could. The island ponies were only half-wild and used to being herded and cared for. The storm would be enough to keep them in the barn through the night, and should there be high water, they would not be caught inside. He then walked quickly to the back door, across the porch, and into the kitchen. He could just see Rachel's long skirts folded in upon one another as she sat on the parlor sofa.

He had been louder than he thought, for as he entered the kitchen Rachel rose and came to the archway that separated the two rooms, her long hair combed tightly back into a soft, wide rope, which even now made her look many years younger than she was. She was mysteriously his own, this woman whom he had hurt and forgotten about these last days and weeks. It seemed impossible to him. Others might do such, but he had rescued her, that young, vulnerable, and deeply muted girl from a family unable to care for her and a father unable to love her. He had wanted it to be a holy mystery, their love. Peter took his wife in his arms and pressed her close to him, as if flesh itself were not alive. For an instant he was afraid that she might leave him.

"Rachel, Rachel!" he said in a deep whisper, ministering to his own deep wounds, "Rachel, I'm so sorry, so very sorry. God forgive, I did not mean to leave you."

"I know, Peter, I know."

His wife's answer proved her real, as did the strong, supple muscles of her back beneath his hands. Rachel was alive, she was alive. He wanted to say something, to repay her for the loneliness of her life, for the burden that he had left for her and for her alone. Instead, he held his wife by the shoulder and walked with her into the parlor. Together they sat upon the sofa, holding one another as if they had been separated for a long while and only now were come home once more.

"And what have they left us, Rachel?" Peter finally said. "What have we here to begin with?"

"They, Peter?" Rachel did not look.

"They, He, God and his angels. What have we left? If it is God's will and if we must obey, then what is left? I'm tired, Rachel. I shall strive no more. I do not believe I have been contentious, yet I shall contend no more." Peter lay heavily against the sofa and put his free arm upon its back. He stared at the green diamond pattern of the wallpaper until the tiny flowers, which anchored the corners of each section and wove them into an intricate repetition of diamond upon diamond, again and again went in, then out, in, then out of focus.

"Where are our monuments, Rachel? What has been left?"

"Peter, my Peter," Rachel cried and thrust her arms around his thick waist, "don't hurt yourself so. If you want monuments, look around you. They're here, everywhere. Oh, my love. What if there were no God? What if this had happened, all our sons again taken from us, and there were no God? Would you feel as you do now? Sometimes I think you would find it easier that way."

"But, Rachel, that's nonsense. Are you saying that I don't believe?"

"No, of course not." Rachel pressed her head to his breast and would not look at him. "Oh, Peter, it seems that I have loved you and you have taught me and given me strength all my life. Yet Peter, you—" Rachel's head pressed even harder against his chest. "Please don't hate me, Peter, please don't. It's just that we've never been able to live up to you. Maybe God's never lived up to you either. Not up to what you expected of Him."

For the second time that day, Peter could not find anything to say. What if there were no God? He had never considered that, yet the answer seemed childishly simple. If there were no God, then life held no meaning. That was child's play, something a freshman theology student at Hampton-Sydney could have proved in a moment and been bored in the process.

Even enlightened hedonism eventually led to metaphysical cynicism and despair. It was a blind alley (Peter smiled), a dead fish.

But the corollary he had forgotten. If there was a God, then meaning was essential to life, to death too, essential and inevitable, for life would be meaning, God's meaning and God's mysterious will. It was inevitable, a final piece in a puzzle he had been working out for generations.

"Oh, Peter, we can't bribe God with goodness. It won't make any difference. It was just an accident, what happened; our boys dying was an accident. God's accident. It won't ever happen again this way, but this once it has, and we've got to accept it."

"I know, Rachel. I think I know that." Peter stroked the long, thick strands of his wife's hair as it lay across her back. Nothing seemed as important to him now as making her happy once more, giving her comfort.

"And we're not alone, Peter." Rachel pulled away from him and held his hard, dirty hands in hers. "You know that too, don't you?"

"Yes, I guess I know that."

"We've loved those boys these last years as much as any mother and father could. We've loved them and cared for them and cried over them, and that's not gone. It's going to be with us always, Peter, always. It can never be gone. Not even death can take it from us."

Love once enacted remains. An act, once committed, is immutable for all time. Peter recited elementary logic to himself, but that wasn't all. No. Love endured, not just as act but as feeling. Love remained because it was in and of itself good. How he loved this woman beside him now. How could he tell her how much he loved her? How had he ever done so before? Once enacted, love remained; once felt, love endured. Hardly as many had died here as on Ezekiel's fantastic ship that came across the ocean. Would he have had Rachel and himself die and leave the boys alone? One lived with what remained, and that was always enough.

"Peter, it's getting late." Rachel's voice broke in upon him.

"The light's fading, Rachel. It's to be a long, cold night."

"Then we'd best hurry to the Midgetts' before we lose our way. They'll be keeping supper for us."

The two sat silently for a long moment before Peter went into the kitchen to wash quickly and dress. Even though Rachel reminded him that they were late for Abigail's dinner, he felt no urgency. Both of them were tired but without discomfort. The long tension that they had lived through the past months was over. They were released.

Rachel lit a candle and went upstairs to fetch Peter a clean shirt and pressed trousers. His boots would do. It was bound to rain before long. When she came down, the upstairs windows were shuttered, and while Peter dressed in the kitchen, she checked the rest of the house. As he tightened his belt, Peter heard her call from the front door.

"Peter, Peter come here!"

He tucked in his shirt and walked into the hall to the door.

"What on earth is this, Peter? Where could it have possibly come from?"

Her hair blown by the wind through the open door, Rachel held Ezekiel's painting, balancing it upright on the floor. In the dim candlelight of the hallway it lost its magic and seemed only some ugly and distracted confusion of colors flung together one upon the other without purpose or thought.

"Why, it's Ezekiel's painting, the one I saw the night before last and talked to him about yesterday. What's it doing here?"

"Don't ask me, Peter Wahab." Rachel grimaced as she spoke and peered at the canvas. "I've not such learning about these things. But if he wanted to give it to you, why didn't he knock for me instead of leaving it out there on the porch where the wind and weather could get at it? Seems mighty odd. I'm no stranger to Ezekiel."

"Gabriel said that earlier today Ezekiel was carrying that around asking for me and refusing to show it to anyone."

"It's strange, then, that he should be so careless with it now."

"He must have wanted me to keep it for him."

Peter walked over to Rachel and took the big painting from her. He wanted to look at it some more, but not now. They were already late for supper. "I'll put it in the parlor, and we can decide what to do with it in the morning." Peter stood the painting up against a wall and went to get Rachel's wrap. Putting it around her shoulders, he pulled on his own jacket and hurried her out the door.

The Midgetts were waiting for them when they arrived, and Abigail calmed Rachel's protestations with "Oh, we knew you'd be a bit late, so I began late and took my own time about it. Never could get that man of yours around on time." Gabriel took the coats and pushed, almost shoved, Peter into the parlor.

"Sit down and let the women worry a mite. You look a sight cleaner than you did this afternoon."

"That's what a woman will do for a man, scrub his ears and plaster his hair."

Gabriel laughed roundly and poked at the logs in the fireplace. "It's goin' to be a cold, wet night, Peter, but this one don't look as bad as the last."

"Might snow."

"Aye, it might at that. Wake up those northerners for sure. They've probably never seen it snow at sea."

"It'll be mighty hard on that old palmetto, Gabriel," Abigail lectured her husband as she and Rachel came in from the hall. "You can use your time better than to sit around here wishin' snow on us when we've already got enough cold to last into next winter."

"I wasn't wishin' any such thing, woman, but don't you use that as an excuse for a cold supper." Gabriel winked at Peter. "Old Job's tree has lived through a lot worse than this, though that's about all you can say for it. Needs to be cut down, I suspect, don't you think, Peter?"

"Uprooted and sent south." Peter smiled.

"You'll do no such thing with my tree, Peter Wahab, no such thing," Rachel joined in. "Lord-a-mercy, you haven't got a grain of sand in your head—or maybe that's all—just sand. That tree comes back every spring along about the time the bayonet plants bloom. Trouble with you men is you just work and eat, work and eat. A body'd think you never saw anything pretty in your entire life."

"Workin' and eatin's enough to do on these islands. Takes a full day to be sure of that." Gabriel looked over at his wife. "Do we eat soon, Abigail, or shall poor Peter here faint away from hunger?"

"Gabriel Midgett, stop that!" Rachel answered.

Abigail smoothed her dress before rising. She raised her eyebrows to her husband. "I imagine you'll both wait your turn. Haven't seen one of you yet faint from exhaustion on a winter's day."

Gabriel put the screen in front of the fireplace, and the three followed his wife into the dining room. Abigail served hot soup and brought in a whole smoked ham for her husband to carve. At one point Peter could not help remarking that the china looked just like the kind Job had once given his mother. "A very beautiful pattern, Abigail, to use on such an ordinary occasion."

"Well, it's not Pharaoh's, Peter, if that's what you think," Abigail bantered good-naturedly, "but it's due to him that we have it. My mother had your uncle order this direct from England years ago."

"That's right, Abigail, and if my husband had bothered to look before in these last twenty years, he'd have noticed," said Rachel.

"Well, Peter, now we know you're not one for fine china, don't we?" Gabriel laughed and then they all did. Peter realized that he had not laughed for a long time.

Gabriel told old stories over the table. One by one they heard them and laughed at them as they had laughed before. Ann Bonny and Mary Read strode across pirates' decks. "And the Flaming Ship of Ocracoke, we cannot forget her, Peter. She comes back on lonely, sea-dark nights to haunt us all."

"Listen to him," Abigail chided, "a man who knows all the stories—every one and makes up half as many more—yet couldn't find his way out of the inlet or over the Sound if he had Porpoise Sal herself to show him the way."

"Why, Abigail, you can't spread such rumors about me here," Gabriel said. "It was my father and I who taught that porpoise all she knows, and year by year she comes back to rechart the shoals for us and show us every spring what the winter has wrought."

Porpoise Sal—Peter wondered if she really did exist. He'd never seen her, and yet the animal was a legend on the Core Banks, an amazing porpoise-woman who had lived down south on Cape Lookout in an old, deserted city. It was absurd, but Gabriel swore he'd seen her.

"Ah, she's a good friend of mine, Peter. My wife's a bit jealous I'm not with her as often as with Sal."

"How you do talk big for a landbound sailor, Mr. Midgett. You've got your porpoises awry, my good man. Hatteras Jack guides our ships, not Sal, who was lost out on Diamond Shoals."

"Lost she was." Gabriel showed no sign of his mistake.

"Right off Diamond City when a thousand and more porpoises came to receive her home after so many years among us. She went, too, and now patrols these waters just as Hatteras Jack used to before he passed away." Gabriel affected an exaggerated bereavement, putting his hand over his heart and rolling his eyes toward the ceiling. "Trouble with you, old gal, is you don't know the difference yet between a boy and a girl."

Rachel unsuccessfully tried to smother a guffaw with her hand. Gabriel himself couldn't keep from smiling.

"Well, I'll be—" Abigail militantly rose from the table. "We'll let you keep the rest of your stories for the men at the station. Porpoises may be a different thing, old man, but by now I well know the difference, believe me. You've seen to that well enough! Now it's time to let these good folks get home before the storm breaks. It's after ten and a wonder they've stayed this long with you carryin' on so."

Still chuckling, Gabriel rose from the table and followed his guests and his wife into the hallway.

"Thank you all so for having us by, Abigail," Rachel said as she put on her wrap. "It was so good to be about again."

"Oh, it was nothing at all, you just forget about it. I guess if you can put up with Gabriel you're worth invitin' over again, too. Now you take care, you hear? It's a mean night out." Gabriel opened the door.

"I suspect Peter will be back, Abigail. He was hungry some, all right. You almost ate that ham all by yourself, Peter."

"Listen who's talkin' here. Good night and take care."

The door closed, and Peter and Rachel walked quickly through the yard gate and out onto the road. Rachel pulled her cape tighter about her neck.

"You should have worn your coat," Peter said. "Winter is no time to worry about ladies' fashions."

"I've never seen Gabriel so jolly, Peter. Did you notice it?" Rachel ignored him and went on about more important things. "There are some things these islands give we're very lucky to have. Friends like Gabriel and Abigail is one of them."

"Yes, you're right." The wind swirled and Peter leaned against it, holding Rachel by the waist as he did so. The dry sand was difficult to walk in, and he guided her onto the grass fringe of the road. "It's one of the reasons Gabriel makes such a good coastguardsman. He knows people, when to laugh and when to be serious." Had Gabriel been right that afternoon to imply that he himself would have made a good storekeeper?

"Peter?"

"Yes?"

Rachel's voice had grown wary. "Peter, I want to be serious for a minute, too."

"What is it?"

Rachel stopped. She gripped his hand and looked up at him through the wind.

"Peter, we're going by the cemetery on the way home. Just a step from it. There isn't much there now. Nothing you can see. Would you take me there for a moment? Just a moment, Peter, and then you'll never have to come back again. I'll never ask it of you."

Peter looked down at his wife. He could see little of her face in the darkness. He wondered if she were crying.

"Yes," he said, "I'll go with you."

They walked on together silently and took the little path that led to the back of the cemetery lot. The great live oak moaned heavily as they walked under it and made their way to the roadside through a winter's tangle of bushes. They stopped in front of the white rope. It was too dark to see anything at a distance, yet neither had intended to go into the cemetery. They stood for a brief time, holding one another's hand and staring into the night.

"I had expected it to be different, Rachel," Peter said huskily. "I had expected some great change before I would feel this way. A miracle, thunder maybe, a bolt of lightning from the sky. I wanted something, and nothing ever really came. Even that painting of Ezekiel's now doesn't seem so much. It just all came so slowly. My boys are dead."

"It's over, Peter. Come back to me again as I remember you. Take me home now. It's right cold out here."

Peter gathered his wife against him and walked slowly up the road beneath the approaching storm. At the cottage the gate swung open abruptly as the wind tore it from his grasp. This was home, he thought. God, this was his home!

# XVI

# EPILOGUE

*And there shall be no night there:
and they need no candle....*

FOR ALL ITS FEROCITY, winter comes slowly to the Banks, and except during a storm, it is never fully distinguished from late fall or early spring. The yaupon keeps its leafage all year round, as do the live oak and cedar. The days build one upon another far out to sea and then move inland to visit the islands beneath them. It is this very movement of cloud and wind that is most apparent and therefore a reliable indicator of season. During the late spring, summer, and early fall, the predominant winds are from the southeast. Sometimes the Caribbean high moves up over Georgia and the Carolinas, bringing with it hot, burning days; but the evenings bring cooling breezes, which generate in the hundreds of miles of swamp across the Sound or in the Gulf Stream. By evening these breezes stiffen into strong, yet warm winds that at times blind those who walk the beach late at night with the sand that the winds scoop up from the beach and carry out to sea. Only when there is a hurricane moving up the coast do these winds ever change to the east, and this is usually in the fall, thus mitigating an untoward or unseemly change.

By December, however, the predominant winds blow from the north and northeast, bringing with them the iciness of barren Canadian tundra. All through December, January, February, and March, these winds remain supremely fickle. Often the morning will begin with clouds moving ponderously out to sea only to have them racing inland by noon as another nor'easter pushes down from the Atlantic Ocean, spawned by the shifting Labrador Current and the vagrancies of the open sea. Shut tight, the islands wait in patient solitude.

Now and then a winter coot will break suddenly from his nest and squawk loudly into the air. The Banks are the winter resting place for all kinds of ducks and geese: Canadian, black, pintail, wood, widgeon, teal, scaup, and many others stay throughout January on into March. With the summer residents gone, the islands become eerily silent and naked. Only the thin, hollow calls of the birds are heard far up and down the long, slender stretches of marshes that still remain on the Sound side.

Peter awoke next morning to such a sound. He stretched, shook the sleep from his head, and walked to the window.

The storm had not come, he noted without surprise. Clouds were tirelessly rolling over the island from the mainland, and it was merely a matter of which storm would push the other away, bringing its own special harrowing to the Banks. In any case, the islands lived for the moment within the tension, and this day would be one in which some work could be done before the battle was decided. There were the ponies to be looked after and wood to be cut and stashed under the porch. Gabriel had briefly mentioned some roofing that needed mending, and Peter wanted to help his friend if he could. And finally, there was Ezekiel. If possible, Peter wanted to find the old Negro early in the day and make sure he was in good health and taken care of. He felt poorly about the way he'd treated Ezekiel two nights before and was worried that the old man might take to heart his previous anger.

Rachel rose early as well. Peter went into the parlor and looked at the painting for a while. It was beautiful after all. Then the two ate breakfast before he went into the barn to look after the ponies.

The lame mares were huddled together in a far corner and submitted docilely to his inspection. The yearling, however, kept to itself and wouldn't let Peter touch him. Around and around the barn he chased it, making sure the door was shut, once tripping over his own feet as he tried to follow the pony's quick movements here and there within the enclosed space. All the while the mares remained as passive as ever, seemingly amused by the spectacle of Peter, half on his hands and knees, half on his feet, chasing the colt to first this corner, then that, this, then that. After both had worked up a sweat, Peter finally cornered the colt and haltered him. When looking at the cut upon the animal's back, however, he discovered that it was not as bad as he had previously thought. True, it was red and sore, probably the reason the pony was so adamant about not being touched, but the infection was as yet slight and could be treated easily.

Peter stepped away from an awkward kick and tied the pony's halter to an upright. While he finished cleaning and disinfecting the wound, the pony stood quietly and let Peter do his will. Then Peter saddled his own mount, went into the house to tell Rachel he would be gone for part of the afternoon, and opened the barn doors to let the animals out. The two mares were content to stay and he let them remain, knowing that the older horses would wander north if they left the barn and eventually rejoin the herd. The colt ran out immediately, stopped, took a quick survey of the yard, then headed out the gate toward the center of town. Peter mounted and followed him, finally turning the animal northward before he reached the bay. He continued to guide the pony up the island for many miles.

When the animal was far enough north, Peter left him and turned his own mount toward the east shore. He was certain the yearling would join one of the foraging herds, and Peter wanted to return by way of the beach in order to find Ezekiel if the old man happened to be near. The breeze slapped at his face and clothing as he rode onto the open sand and turned south. It was a cold, raw day, and Peter was glad he'd dressed warmly before leaving.

"Two sets of underwear, Peter Wahab," Rachel had said before breakfast, "and a good, hot meal. Don't you go haulin' up and down the island on a day like this without being good and warm. Don't you dare."

And his luck held to starboard, too, for as the pony cantered quickly over the wet, hard sand, he saw Ezekiel on his knees far down the shore, near where the old *Home* had been. Peter spurred his mount and reached the spot where Ezekiel, intent upon his castle, had failed to notice him riding up.

"Why, Mr. Peter. What you doin' out here on a day like today?" Ezekiel called out and rose when he finally heard Peter dismounting and guiding his horse under the lee of a dune.

"Hello, Ezekiel. Just harryin' a pony I tended to overnight up toward the Point. And what might you be up to out here when it's fixin' to storm all creation?"

"Oh, you know better, Mr. Peter. Storm won't come for some time yet. It's laid out to leeward." Ezekiel faced the ocean and looked far away across the horizon. "She's gotta come all the way back in again, and I reckon she'll take her time about it. She'll peel the green when she does, though. I make it tonight, maybe on to mornin' sometime."

"That still doesn't answer what you're up to."

The demand changed the tone of the conversation and made Ezekiel shy. He looked around, down at the sand. "Why, I'm just funnin', Mr. Peter. Just messin' around a bit like any old nigger do now and then."

But the castle was complex, many turreted, and severely bastioned. The sand lay in high clusters where Ezekiel had failed in his hopes, yet each pile was recognizable as part of the whole. Peter felt as though he ought to help build them back, to carry water for the old man in that absurdly leaky pail or dig deeper for wetter sand, which would stabilize the dry, shifting structures that were constantly being torn and eaten by the wind. But he did not.

"You'll never get it finished, Ezekiel, not even if you take all day."

Ezekiel looked up, then back to the castle in mock discouragement. "And half the night, too, I reckon. But maybe tomorrow, Mr. Peter. Maybe tomorrow."

Peter decided to get on with it. Sand castles would keep for warm, summer nights. Here and now he must talk with the old man, find out what, if anything, was bothering him yesterday, and get him off the beach. It was on toward noon, and he still had to see Gabriel.

"I'm going to keep your painting for you, Ezekiel, unless you want it back."

Ezekiel, who had sat down again next to the castle, looked up and smiled. "No, sir. That picture's yours, right and proper. You go ahead and keep it."

"Gabriel says you were looking all over town for me yesterday."

"Yes, sir, but you wasn't nowhere around. I didn't find hide nor hair of you."

"Anything wrong, Ezekiel? Where'd you sleep last night?"

"No, sir. Ain't nothin' wrong with this old man." Ezekiel flexed his arms and inflated his lungs with a deep, audible breath. "No, sir. I'm fine, fit as a fiddle."

"You weren't at the Midgetts' last night. Pickin's must have been mighty sparse."

"No, sir. I found myself a big ole conch on 'bout evenin' and cooked myself up a good stew. Wasn't no need to bother Mr. Midgett."

"Well, for heaven's sake, man, where'd you sleep?" Peter noted that there wasn't anyone better at avoiding questions than Ezekiel.

"Why, in your barn, Mr. Peter. I thought you knowed, the way you talked. I was there when you brought them ponies in, only you didn't take no notice so I let you be."

Peter shook his head. He'd just gathered the ponies in the barn that night and never even looked around.

"I tried to help that yearlin', Mr. Peter, didn't you see? Lord, he was a sassy one. Almost kicked me black and blue, he did."

"Well, I'll be— Was that you, Ezekiel?" Peter felt foolish. Of course the wound had been cared for, hardly well or adequately, but he couldn't have been that wrong about it the day before.

"Yes, sir, sure was. I hauled on out of there bright and early this mornin' to get up here. Had work to do, lots of work on days like today."

Lots of work—the old man lived in another world. "I suppose you're goin' to try and paint the old *Home* sometime soon, Ezekiel, that right?" Evidently the old Negro was fine. He had probably left the painting at the front door before going around back into the barn. Most likely, he hadn't wanted to disturb Rachel, and after all, it was their painting, Ezekiel's and his. It was an exotic and strangely incomplete prophecy, one never to be preached before the multitude. Peter wanted to joke a little. His fears had been for naught. The old man was fine.

"No *Home* out there, Mister Peter," Ezekiel said without even looking. "Your ship, she all gone. Besides, I don't want to paint any more. I'm through with that."

Ezekiel wanted to talk. It was the same way after every painting he gave away. He wasn't going to paint any more.

"I suppose paints are too hard to come by, Ezekiel. Is that it? No paints, no boards to paint on?"

"No, that ain't it, Mister Peter. Not this time. I'm just tired of it. I'm gettin' too old for that kind of thing. A body's got to slow down sometime."

"Oh, you'll paint some more next year, soon as the winter's out of your bones and your fingers feel loose and free. You say it every year, Ezekiel, and every year you've got another excuse to begin again."

Ezekiel did not try to convince his antagonist; he just stated his conviction. "This time it's for sure, Mr. Peter. I ain't goin' to paint no more. I'm tired, tired like that old ship was, and it's time for me to go home, too."

Peter watched the old man carefully, squinting through the capriciously blown sand. How fine a man this was, the old grizzled beard bleached against the weathered black face. Strong he seemed, and courageous. He had never seen fear on Ezekiel's face, not that he could remember, at least.

"Yes, I gotta be gettin' along, Mr. Peter. I been around too long."

*He it is that doth go before thee,
he will not fail thee, neither forsake thee:
fear not, neither be dismayed.*

Ezekiel began to gather up his belongings.
"But wait, Ezekiel, how can you say that?" Of all things, now he was trying to keep the Negro from leaving. "Why, your painting isn't even finished. Are you going to leave that muddy spot with all the people in it?"

Ezekiel flung his sack back upon the sand, knelt down before the castle, started to build again, and affected a disinterest towards Peter's question. After a while, Peter asked again.

"Well, are you?"

"Oh, I don't know, Mr. Peter. I gotta build my castle. That picture's over and done with."

"But the painting's unfinished, Ezekiel."

"Yes, Mr. Peter, yes. An' it'll most likely stay that way. Don't see how I'll ever do it again."

"Do what, Ezekiel?" Peter moved to the despairing old man and knelt beside him, putting his hands upon his shoulders.

"No, no," Ezekiel just shook him off.

"No, what? I'm your friend, Ezekiel. What's troublin' you so?"

"No, you never can help, Mr. Peter. You never can."

Ezekiel continued to look down at the castle's crumbling turrets.

"What, what is it I can't help, Ezekiel?"

Ezekiel looked up apologetically. Now he didn't want to talk; but the white man was forcing him, and he had no defenses. They were together in grief.

"You remember that nigger Pharaoh once killed, Mr. Peter? You remember him?"

"Only through stories, Ezekiel. Why?"

"He's there somewhere, there in the picture. Don't ask me

where, I don't know, but he's there all right. My mamma—my mamma once tole me that he was my daddy."

"My God."

"I don't know, I don't know, Mr. Peter. My mamma just tole me once. That's all."

Peter let go of Ezekiel's shoulders and sat with him upon the sand.

*I am sought by them that asked not for me;*
*I am found by them that sought me not.*

"It was a sin born out of love, Ezekiel," Peter said after a time in which the Negro continued to work on the castle while Peter sat immobile and watched him.

"My mamma said they loved each other a lot even if they wasn't married. She said that made it all right, that the Lord wouldn't mind none what they did, and besides, she was the daughter of a queen, she said."

Peter watched the old man work. "And that's why Judith left, Ezekiel? That's why. There's nothing to forgive. Pharaoh loved us all too well." It was getting cold, terribly cold. He shivered. Rachel, he thought, would be knitting, strand by strand, warm, woolen clothing on a day like today.

Ezekiel didn't attempt to answer. He had told this man all he could. It was over for him.

"You know she'll never come back," Peter finally said to Ezekiel as the old man moved about the castle walls, poking long stalks of sea oats into the sand outside them. "She'll never come back to you. You know that, don't you?"

"Who, Mr. Peter? Who you mean?" Ezekiel stopped and looked up at him quizzically.

"Deborah, the great queen you build your castles for, she'll never come back. No more than Judith will ever come back. They've both gone."

Ezekiel broke into a broad smile of recognition. "Oh, no,

Mr. Peter. Why, Deborah don't have to come back. She never left." The Negro pointed to his head. "She been here all the time, right up here."

The two rode back to the village together. First one walked and then the other, making slow time of it with Ezekiel's junk affixed to the saddle and hanging awkwardly over the pony's rump. A freak wind opened up a hole in the clouds, however, and all the way back to the village the dazzling sunlight played over them and rippled along the water. Peter was glad of it, for it would have been terribly cold otherwise.

When he arrived home, Ezekiel scurried into the barn with both the pony and his belongings.

"Don't you worry none, Mr. Peter. I'll rub him down for you. You go ahead in and see Miz Rachel. I'll take care of things here."

Peter went into the house and sat down to an already hot dinner with Rachel. When he told her what he'd learned that morning, she caught her breath.

"And we've never known, all these years."

"Never once. I suspect we never finish putting the pieces of our puzzle together, Rachel. There are always more of them and more and more."

"Land sakes. Does he have food? Shouldn't we get him a hot meal? Why didn't you bring him in?"

"He'll be in soon, I'm sure." Peter finished his coffee and pushed back from the table. "I'm off to see Gabriel about that roof of his, and I'll be back around early evening. You take care now."

Peter kissed his wife, pulled on his heavy jacket, and walked toward the door.

"If you need anything here, send Ezekiel to fetch me."

"Keep warm now, Peter Wahab, you hear?" Rachel called after him. "This ain't fit weather."

The work at Gabriel's that afternoon went fast. Peter arrived just as his friend was climbing a ladder which leaned up against the side of the eaves and protruded over the top of the gently sloping roof.

"Well, just in time for what little's left, Peter," Gabriel yelled. "Where were you this mornin' when I could have used you? Ah, you're a latecomer, Peter, a latecomer if ever I saw one."

Peter laughed but did not tell Gabriel about the morning. As the afternoon wore on, he became certain that there was no reason ever to speak of it again. He would hang the picture upstairs. It was enough.

"I'm glad you came, Peter," Gabriel said, taking a nail out of his pocket and with two sure blows driving it into a stud alongside the eave. "It does a man good to get out and work, to work hard and forget about himself. I don't mind telling you I was more than a little worried this last week. It's been a bad time."

Peter sucked his thumb. He had just hit himself with the hammer. "Yes, I believe so. Anyway, it's all behind us. Gabriel?"

"Yes?"

"Do you really need help at the store? How serious were you yesterday?"

Gabriel stopped and thought a moment. "Why, serious as I could be, Peter. After all, the store's part yours, though you've chosen to forget about it all this time. I haven't done a decent inventory in years, and now's the time of the year for one. This station's a full-time job."

"I've some things to tend to round the house for a few days. Would Monday a week be right with you?"

"Why, that'd be fine, Peter, just fine." Gabriel smiled with satisfaction as he spoke. "Abigail will like that, too. She's never taken much to storekeepin'—or workin' on roofs. Yes, that'll be real fine."

Peter smiled against the wind. It was good to be atop the cottage, in the sometimes flickering eye of a winter's sun. The wind was cold and chilling, but he didn't mind. He remembered a dog he had once seen lying in front of the store licking itself. The day had been a sharp, fall day with the rush of colors that only rarely and briefly comes to the Banks. The dog had lain hard up against the rotten boards on an inside corner of the porch and store, vainly trying to protect itself from the wind. It had contentedly, even imperiously, continued to lick itself. All the while Peter stood talking to Gabriel. The seared, red and brown leaves from the old maple fell over and around them, all three; the dog unaware, Peter felt, even of his own action. So long ago.

"Look out there, Peter." Gabriel was grunting with a professional, disinterested contempt. He pointed east, out to sea. "There's another'un. If she don't put in at Hatteras, she'll have a hard night of it."

"She will at that," Peter responded. "But look at how tall and straight those masts sit. She rides well into the wind."

"Aye, but foolishly. It'll be a tricky reach into the harbor. It's the likes of her and such captains that make for salvage on the beach." Gabriel leaned over the roof's edge and spat. "One night like last Saturday is enough. We're not always so lucky."

Peter looked out at the ship. At least it wasn't running before the wind, and those masts did so look like tall, proud trees. A bit too much sail, perhaps, but still— He saw a gull lift high over the shoreline. It held motionless for a moment on the crest of a draft; then arcing into the wind, it fell swiftly and surely toward the sand, disappearing behind the roof of a small, white cottage at the end of the road.

"Ah, the waste of it, Peter." Gabriel was beginning to work again. "But ships will always go out to sea, storm or no storm."

Peter smiled and fitted a shingle into place. The height made him momentarily dizzy. He stared intently at the hard, solid roof to regain himself. "And we must finish the roof, Gabriel, before the gale takes it off."

Gabriel looked at Peter and guffawed. Then they both laughed loudly, feeling that they were children again, playing in some airy retreat with no need to maintain the dignity of their age. It was heady, being untouched by anything except the chill edge of the wind and the warm flood of sunlight. It made the work easy, easy and almost comfortable.

Soon Peter noticed that the clouds were moving swiftly from the northeast again. Ezekiel was right. The storm had been stopped for only a day. The night would bring it for sure. The wind whipped about him and he hurried on with his work.

Long about two or three, Beth Turner came by for Abigail.

"Not here, Beth," Gabriel yelled down. "She's at the store if you want her bad enough."

"Well, I'll be fixed, Gabriel Midgett," Beth called up to them. "Always thinking up excuses for your wife to do your work for you, aren't you? And look at that man next to you. A body'd think you need the whole town just for a simple mending job."

"On with you, on with you, girl. Your material won't be in till the next boat, and what with this weather, who knows when that'll be?"

"I'm going. I'm going, Gabriel. Don't hurry me now."

"Beth?"

"Yes, Peter," Beth smiled up at him.

"Rachel and I'd like you for supper one of these days soon."

"Why, that'd be right nice, Peter. The very minute we get all these outlanders off the island, I'll see Rachel about it. Good evening."

"Goodbye," the two men called together as Beth walked on down the street.

"A blessed angel, that'un," Gabriel said carelessly and went back to his work.

Before they finished late in the afternoon, half the village had passed by, Peter thought. The last man to come was Marcus Hawkins, whom they both tried to ignore, but the good minister would not be denied.

"But I can't," yelled Gabriel in frustration from his perch on the peak of the roof. "Marcus, I can't help you. If the storm lasts into the weekend, I'll be needed at the station all the time. You can see that, can't you?"

"It's a special service this Sunday, Gabriel, for the outlanders. They'll have been here a week, and it's hard on those who aren't used to it. You ought to see them over at the hotel, proggin' around from one place to another like starved cats. We need your help."

Gabriel and Peter both smiled. "They'll eat their fine foods soon enough, and as for special services, let 'em worship our way. It's plain and simple with no nonsense. It'll do 'em good."

Encouraged by the smiles, Marcus would not leave. "Thou shalt not deny thy Lord, Gabriel," he shouted up, waving his fist. "The church is in need of you."

Finally, Peter pacified the worried preacher. "I'll do it for you, Marcus, if Gabriel can't. Just leave the lessons with Rachel when you're able, and I'll read them Sunday. That is, if folks will have me."

"Why, that's mighty kind of you, Peter." Marcus Hawkins began playing with his cuffs and coat sleeves. "Yes—yes, that will certainly more than do. A fine gesture, what with— I'll be by soon now. Take care."

The two men watched the disappearing preacher and finished their work in silence. The clouds were darker now and full with rain. Both wanted to be done before the storm broke.

Out to sea, the ocean swelled in furious bursts of energy, goaded by the wind above it. The sky was black and the water a deep, angry gray. There were no other ships at sea now in such weather, and none would put out. Ports were closed, boats beached and tied down, ships hove to and anchored. Northward, Currituck was becoming muddy, while to the west the wide reaches of Pamlico Sound were empty and noiseless.

Rachel Wahab sang softly as she went about her work. Ezekiel, she knew, was upstairs sleeping. There were so many empty rooms in the house, and the old man seemed so tired, so very tired after his afternoon walk. It had been nice of him, too, sweet of him, to bring back the holly, the wonderful redolent sprigs of beach holly that she was now arranging on the parlor sideboard. She looked out at the palmetto and then back at the holly. How good it was to have color in the house. The holly was so gay, so—

But, she reminded herself, Peter would be home soon. The wind was picking up. The windows shuddered as a strong flaw whistled about them. There was much to be done. Supper must be looked to. Peter would be chilled to the bone. And she must put out or bank the fires just to be safe. She stopped and listened. No, Ezekiel was still asleep. He would eat with her and Peter that night, she decided. The dear old man couldn't take care of himself any more. And then there were the candles, too, she'd almost forgotten. She must light candles against the falling of night.